Till Death
Do Us Part

Alone, April felt the gloom return. It would be another couple of hours before her parents would arrive. *Stop acting like a baby,* she told herself. *This isn't like before. You're seventeen now, not five.*

She was sitting up in her bed clicking through the TV channels with the remote control when someone rapped on her door. "Come in," she called.

The door slowly opened, and the boy from the rec room stood there. "Hi," he said with a sunny grin.

"Do I know you?" she asked.

"Mark Gianni." He held out his hand.

She took it cautiously. His grip was warm, his palm rough. He was tall and had curling dark brown hair and intense deep brown eyes. But Kelli had been right. He was thin, almost gaunt. "And you're here because . . . ?" She allowed the sentence to trail.

"Because I want you to know that you're the most beautiful girl I've ever seen. And I thought I should introduce myself. I mean, we should get to know each other. Since you're the girl I intend to marry."

TURN TO THE BACK OF THIS BOOK FOR A SNEAK PREVIEW OF
For Better, for Worse, Forever,
the companion to *Till Death Do Us Part.*

Lurlene McDaniel

Till Death Do Us Part

BANTAM BOOKS
NEW YORK • TORONTO • LONDON • SYDNEY • AUCKLAND

RL 5.6, ages 012 and up

TILL DEATH DO US PART

A Bantam Book / July 1997

The Starfire logo is a registered trademark of Bantam Books, a division of Bantam Doubleday Dell Publishing Group, Inc. Registered in U.S. Patent and Trademark Office and elsewhere.

For information address: Bantam Doubleday Dell Books for Young Readers, New York, New York 10036.

ISBN 0-553-57085-4

Published simultaneously in the United States and Canada

Bantam Books are published by Bantam Books, a division of Bantam Doubleday Dell Publishing Group, Inc. Its trademark, consisting of the words "Bantam Books" and the portrayal of a rooster, is Registered in U.S. Patent and Trademark Office and in other countries. Marca Registrada. Bantam Books, 1540 Broadway, New York, New York 10036.

PRINTED IN THE UNITED STATES OF AMERICA

OPM   10 9 8 7 6 5 4 3 2 1

This book is lovingly dedicated
to Jennifer Dailey,

a victim of cystic fibrosis a lovely flower,
plucked up by the angels after fourteen years
on this earth, March 12, 1997.
Dear Jennifer, your family and friends will miss you.
May your walk in heaven be joyous!

"Love is patient, love is kind. It does not envy, it does not boast, it is not proud, it is not rude, it is not self-seeking, it is not easily angered, it keeps no record of wrongs. Love does not delight in evil but rejoices with the truth. It always protects, always trusts, always hopes, always perseveres. Love never fails . . ." (1 Corinthians 13:4–8, New International Version)

1

"That guy's staring at you again, April."

April Lancaster didn't need Kelli to tell her that the boy on the far side of the hospital's patient rec room was looking at her. She could almost *feel* his gaze. She had been in the hospital for two days and he'd been stealing glances at her every time she ventured out of her room. "Ignore him," April whispered to Kelli. "I do."

"But why? He's cute. Even if he is too skinny for my taste."

"This isn't a social club, Kelli. It's a hospital. I didn't come here to meet guys."

"Well, I say why let a good opportunity slip away?"

April shook her head. "You're impossible."

Her best friend grinned. "I'm only trying to cheer you up. Take your mind off this whole thing. And if you meet a cute guy in the bargain, then what's the harm?"

April pointedly twisted in the lounge chair so that her back was to the boy. She didn't want to be stared at, and she certainly didn't want to meet some guy who was sick. She figured he had to be sick; why else would he be a patient in this huge New York City medical complex?

Kelli interrupted her thoughts. "What is going on with you? Medically, I mean. When can you leave?"

The last thing April wanted to do was dwell on the frightening possibilities as to why she was in the hospital. "I'm only here for testing," she said. "I'm sure I'll be out by the end of the week."

"But by then spring break will be over. We leave tomorrow, and the weatherman said an inch of fresh powder is falling in Vermont as we speak. This might be the last chance for a ski trip this year."

April and her friends had been planning the trip for weeks. It was supposed to be part of her birthday present. And since it was their senior year, it would be their final spring break together as a group. "I can't help it," she said gloomily. "Even if my doctor releases me earlier, my parents won't let me go."

"Why not?"

April didn't want to say. Not while there was so much speculation about the origins of her numbing headaches. The headaches had built in intensity for the past several months, causing her to get dizzy, even sick to her stomach. When she'd passed out from the pain in school two days earlier, her parents had hustled her out of their Long Island community and into a hospital in the city. The headaches could still be nothing.

Or they could be the other thing. The "thing" she had decided *not* to discuss with Kelli. "Oh, you know my parents. They fall to pieces if I have a hangnail. Besides, Dad won't let me drive from New York to Vermont by myself."

Kelli chewed her bottom lip. "I could wait till you're released. Then you and I could drive up together."

"No way." April shook her head. "Kelli, I appreciate it, but you go on with the others."

Kelli slumped in her chair, crossed her arms,

and pouted. "It won't be the same without you there. This is our last spring break together."

April sighed, feeling disappointed too. "Maybe we can do something together our first spring break from college next year."

"Fat chance. We'll all be scattered to the ends of the earth."

"I'm sorry," April said softly, her eyes filling with tears.

Kelli scooted forward and seized April's hands. "Don't cry. I'm such a jerk for making you feel worse than you already do. Tell you what, we'll go to the shore this summer when all this is behind you. You've always liked the beach better than the ski slopes anyway. I'll talk to the others while we're away and devise a plan. What do you say?"

"Okay. Maybe we can go right after graduation, before we have to pack up for college." April did love the beach, the rolling ocean waves, the warm sand and bright sun. "Thanks for thinking of it, Kelli. You're a real friend."

Kelli beamed her a smile. "We'll call you from the ski lodge."

April nodded. "*Don't* break a leg."

Suddenly a male voice burst upon the two girls in the lounge. "There you are, April."

April looked up to see Chris Albright, the senior captain of their high-school soccer team. They'd been dating for a few months, ever since Christmas, but she hadn't expected him to pop into the hospital the day before spring break. She was glad she'd taken the time to put on her sweats and wasn't wearing a hospital gown.

"I couldn't find you in your room," Chris continued. "One of the nurses told me to check in here. You feeling better?"

Chris had caught her when she'd fainted in English class. Literally.

"Nothing to report," she said. He straddled the arm of her chair and took her hand in his. From the corner of her eye, April saw the patient who'd been ogling her lean forward. She turned her full attention to Chris. "I didn't think I'd see you until after the break."

"I can't go off and leave my girlfriend holed up in the hospital."

Kelli, who was out of Chris's line of vision, did an exaggerated swoon that made April giggle. Chris was the catch of their school. April was nuts about him, but she tried not to show it. Clingy girlfriends were a turnoff.

"What's so funny?" Chris asked.

"Nothing. I'm just glad to see you." She laced her fingers through his.

"What's up, Kelli?" Chris asked.

"I came to say goodbye too," Kelli told him. "Actually I was trying to persuade April to sneak away with me and leave her doctor a note about coming back after spring break."

"Makes sense to me," Chris said. "Have they told you anything yet?"

April told Chris what she'd told Kelli. Once again she omitted the information that she didn't want anyone to know. *The headaches can't be related,* she told herself. "So, I guess I'm stuck here until they complete all the tests," she finished aloud.

"What kind of doctor have you got?" Chris wanted to know.

"A neurologist." She leaned forward. "Personally, I think all this is a ploy to find out if I really have a brain."

Kelli rolled her eyes and Chris scoffed. "Right," he said. "You're on the dean's list every reporting period. I don't think brain loss is your problem."

They all laughed and April felt better. More than anything she wanted to be out of the hospital and back in the familiar world of school and friends and graduation plans. Graduation was only nine weeks away. *Stupid headaches!*

"Listen, I'd better run," Kelli said, standing. "I want to catch the train before rush hour."

"Thanks for visiting." April longed to be leaving with her friend.

"I'll call you." Kelli bent and hugged her goodbye. She whispered in April's ear, "I know three's a crowd," and darted out the door.

Chris eased into Kelli's vacated chair. "I miss you, April."

"I miss you too."

"You scared everybody when you blacked out in class."

"Did I ever thank you for catching me before I hit the floor?"

He glanced self-consciously around the room. "Is there any place less public than here?"

"My room."

"Let's go." He helped her to her feet.

The room spun and she clung to him. "It takes me a minute to get my balance whenever I change positions."

He looked concerned and put his arm around her waist. As they walked back to her room, April felt the gaze of the guy on the far side of the lounge area following them. She snuggled closer to Chris.

Once they were in the privacy of her room, Chris took her in his arms and kissed her. "I hate to leave you for a whole week." The soccer team was playing a tournament in Pennsylvania over the break.

"Go have a good time. But not too good a time."

He stayed for another hour before he kissed her goodbye.

Alone, she felt the gloom return. It would be another couple of hours before her parents would arrive. *Stop acting like a baby,* she told herself. *This isn't like before. You're seventeen now, not five.*

She was sitting up in her bed clicking through the TV channels with the remote control when someone rapped on her door. "Come in," she called.

The door slowly opened, and the boy from the rec room stood there. "Hi," he said with a sunny grin.

"Do I know you?" she asked.

"Mark Gianni." He held out his hand.

She took it cautiously. His grip was warm, his palm rough. He was tall and had curling dark brown hair and intense deep brown eyes. But Kelli had been right. He was thin, almost gaunt. "And you're here because . . . ?" She allowed the sentence to trail.

"Because I want you to know that you're the most beautiful girl I've ever seen. And I thought I should introduce myself. I mean, we should get to know each other. Since you're the girl I intend to marry."

2

Although Mark's bold statement shocked April, she refused to let him see her reaction. Without changing her expression, she asked, "And what makes you think I'm not already married?"

Mark looked surprised. But suddenly, an impish grin crossed his face. "No ring," he said, picking up her left hand. "If a guy was married to you, he'd make you wear a ring the size of a baseball. And wouldn't your last name be different from your parents'?"

She tugged her hand out of his. "I don't believe in changing my name." Her eyes narrowed. "And how do you know my last name anyway?"

"I asked the nurses. They said you're April Lancaster and you live on the Island."

She wasn't sure she liked him knowing anything about her without her permission. "Well, they shouldn't have told you anything."

"Don't be mad at them. I've been coming here for years, so I know most of the nurses really well. They like me." He grinned again. "I'll bet you could like me too if you gave me a chance."

His smile was infectious and though she tried to hide it, the corners of her mouth twitched. "Well, I'm not here looking for a husband, thank you."

He shrugged. "Okay, so maybe my proposal was a little premature. I'll ask again once we get to know each other better." Suddenly Mark ducked his head and began coughing deeply into his hand. When the coughing fit finally subsided, he looked up and said in a wheezy voice, "Don't worry. I'm not contagious."

She blushed because that was exactly what she had been thinking. "So what are you here for?"

"CF—cystic fibrosis. I was born with it."

She'd heard of the disease but knew nothing about it. "I'm sorry."

With his coughing spasm over, Mark looked paler, and April saw dark circles under his brown eyes. "Can I sit? I feel a little woozy."

Quickly, she pulled her knees up to allow him room to ease onto her bed. "You all right? Should I call a nurse?"

"I'm all right." His smile was less bold, more wavering, and his sudden vulnerability touched her. "A person learns to live with it. Sometimes CF gets the upper hand and then I have to come here until I get on top of it."

"How often do you get hospitalized?"

"It depends. When I was a kid, I sometimes came three or four times a year. But now that I'm older, I'm doing better. This is only my second time in eighteen months."

"How do you stand it? I hate this place."

"So do I. But I don't have a choice. Randy, my RT—that's respiratory therapist—made me come this time." Mark waved his hand. "But enough of this boring stuff, let's talk about something more interesting—like you, for instance. Why are you here?"

"Testing." Talking to him had made her

forget her problems for the moment, and she hated the reminder.

"Well, they can't be testing for imperfections. You're already perfect."

She rolled her eyes. "Do you ever get results with such lame lines?"

"Ouch! I'm wounded. How could you think I'm feeding you a line?"

"Oh puh-leeze. It's been fun meeting you, but don't I hear the dinner trays?"

Out in the hall there was the unmistakable clatter of the cart carrying the supper trays for the patients. April's door swung open and an orderly carried in a beige plastic tray with plates covered by stainless steel domes. He set it down on her bedside table.

"You got room 423 on that cart still?" Mark asked.

"Yes," the orderly answered.

"Can you bring it in here?" Before April could say anything, Mark turned his beautiful eyes on her. "Would you mind?" he asked shyly. "Eating alone is really a downer."

Instantly, April realized why Mark acted like such a flirt. He was lonely. "Only if you promise not to use any more dumb lines on me."

His grin turned sunny again. "Nothing dumb about them. I work hard to perfect them. After all, it's not easy for me to compete with guys who are healthy."

The orderly plunked Mark's tray on the table in the corner and left. Mark lifted her tray and put it across the table from his. "Dinner is served," he said in a snooty voice.

She joined him, but before she could take a bite, she saw him take a medicine cup full of pills. "What are the pills for?"

"CF is a disease of the pancreas. It affects the lungs and also digestion. I have to take pills before every meal to help me digest food. But why are we talking about me again? I'd rather talk about you."

She made up her mind to ask a nurse more about CF. "I'm a dull subject."

"Not to me. Is that guy who I saw you with earlier your boyfriend?"

"Yes." She wanted Mark to know she was unavailable.

"I'll bet he's a jock."

"He plays soccer."

"When I'm on top of my CF, I play chess." He grinned. "Bet I could take him in chess."

"Maybe." April suppressed a smile. She

hated to admit it, but Mark's charm was getting to her.

"Are you in school?"

"A senior. And you?"

"I graduated three years ago," he said. "I take night classes at NYU and I work in a print shop. My uncle owns it. My father's a cop and Mom . . . well, Mom lives to cook huge family dinners and harass my sisters, who aren't married to nice Italian boys yet. Luckily, my sisters and I each have our own apartments."

"How many sisters do you have?"

His smile lit up his eyes. "Just two—both older. So how about you?" he asked. "Brothers or sisters?"

"I'm an only."

"Makes sense." He nodded slowly. "I mean, how could they follow an act as beautiful as you?"

"You're getting lame again."

"Sorry. I lost my head." He gave himself a slap on the cheek. "I'm better now."

April smiled in spite of herself. "I have terrific parents. My dad's an investment counselor and my mom's part owner of an antique shop in Manhattan."

"Speaking of antiques, do you like cars?" he asked.

"Cars? Sure."

"I rebuild cars—street rods—as a hobby."

"Street rods?"

"Classic cars from the fifties. We've just finished a fifty-seven Chevy. Aqua and white with white leather upholstery." His eyes sparkled. "The most beautiful thing I've ever seen. Before you, that is."

She ignored his flattery. "And what do you do with the cars after they're rebuilt?"

"We show and sometimes race them."

"Like on a racetrack?"

"Out at the speedway. Ever been there?"

"Uh—no."

"If I'd had a choice about my life, I would have been a race car driver."

"I thought you said you *did* race cars."

"I do, but not the way I'd like to. I'd race as a career."

April realized that Mark's CF probably kept him from such a career. Would she be unable to do the things she wanted to do if something really bad was wrong with her?

"Would you come with me to the track

sometime?" Mark's question pulled her away from her dark thoughts.

"I don't think so."

"Why?"

"You know I'm already dating somebody."

Again the quicksilver smile. "Can't blame me for trying."

A rap on April's door caused both of them to start. A nurse entered. "There you are," she said to Mark, her hands on her hips. "We've been looking for you. It's time for therapy."

Mark rose. "I know, but I was hoping you'd forget."

"No way. Not when you're this close to being released."

"Trying to get rid of me?"

The nurse studied him fondly. "Go see your therapist. He's in your room."

He turned back to April, seized her hand, and planted a kiss on it. "Thanks for the company. I'll be back tomorrow."

"But—"

He was out the door before she could finish.

"I see he finally met you," the nurse said with an amused smile.

"What do you mean?"

"He's been maneuvering an introduction ever since you checked in."

"Is he harmless?"

"Very. In fact, Mark's one of the nicest kids to ever come through these doors."

"What kind of therapy is he supposed to have?"

"Respiratory. CF victims don't have the ability to break down mucus, so it turns thick and gummy and clogs the lung tissue so they can't breathe. The mucus is broken up by medications, inhalants, and by thumping the victim's back and chest several times a day."

"*Every* day?" April asked. Cystic fibrosis sounded awful to her. "For how long? Until his breathing gets better and his cough goes away?"

"If only," the nurse said with a sigh. "No, it's a lifelong thing for him."

"Won't he ever get well?"

The nurse shook her head. "There's no cure for CF. It's one hundred percent fatal."

3

Early the next morning April was brought to the hospital's radiology department. She would spend a portion of the day undergoing X-ray procedures, such as CAT scans and an MRI. Her mother had taken the day off from the store to be with her. April had left her floor while most of the patients were still asleep, so she hadn't seen Mark. But she couldn't forget what the nurse had told her about him.

"Do you know anything about cystic fibrosis?" April asked her mother. April lay on a gurney in the hall outside one of the radiology rooms, waiting for her turn.

"Not much. Why do you ask?"

April's mother was a slim, blond-haired

woman in her mid-forties. She was stylishly and expensively dressed, perfectly groomed, and smelled of expensive perfume. The two of them had always been close, probably because Janice Lancaster had endured medical hell in order to conceive a child. April knew that her parents had spent thousands of dollars on four attempts of in vitro fertilization before she'd been conceived.

She knew her parents loved her, but sometimes she felt as if she were being smothered by them. They showered her with material goods and made certain that she had every advantage. She was their princess and they treated her like one.

Kelli once told April that she couldn't believe she was so down-to-earth and not spoiled rotten. April was kind and sensitive, almost mushy, actually. She cried over sad songs, wounded animals, and even TV commercials. When she was little, she'd cried for days after seeing the movie *Bambi*, because Bambi's mother had been killed and the fawn had been orphaned.

Now, looking back, she suspected that what had happened to her when she was five contributed mightily to the person she had become.

"I met this guy on my floor who has CF," April explained to her mother. "He's sort of goofy, but really nice. Lonely too. A nurse told me that CF is fatal, that it has no cure."

Her mother frowned. "How awful."

"But he doesn't let it get him down. His hobby is rebuilding old cars and racing."

"Sounds dangerous."

Unable to get her mother interested in discussing Mark, April asked, "Mom, do you think the same thing's wrong with me now as when I was five?"

Her mother stiffened and a worried frown settled over her face. Now that the words were out, April could see just how much her headaches and blackout had affected her mother. "That's why we're doing all this testing," her mother said softly. "To rule it out. I personally don't believe the two things are related. They told us then they were sure they had gotten it all." Her mother affectionately tugged April's long thick red hair. "I think we should talk about something else and let these tests tell us what's wrong. No use making up scenarios. So, are your friends on their way to Vermont yet?"

April was disappointed. She wanted to talk about her fears, but it was clear her mother didn't. Perhaps her mother was right. Why get all worked up before the tests results were in? "They left this morning. I'd give anything to be with them."

"I wish you were, honey."

"Kelli said maybe we could all take off for the shore this summer before we go our separate ways."

"That would be nice."

"I like the beach better anyway."

April's doctor came into the waiting area. "How's it going?"

"Okay," April said, mildly surprised to see him in the middle of the day. He usually visited in the evening.

Dr. Sorenson was a big man with a head of white hair and intelligent blue eyes behind black-rimmed glasses. He was wearing scrub greens. "I'm just out of surgery," he said. "I wanted to check on you. See if that medication is working."

April had been taking special pills for three days for the headaches. "It's doing a good job. I haven't had a headache since I got here."

"Maybe April could just take a prescription of the pills and it would straighten her out," her mother suggested.

"We have to know the cause of the headaches," Dr. Sorenson said. "Unless we know why her head hurts, the pills will only be a temporary fix. I'll have more information after the results of today's work."

"When can I go home?"

"Not for another few days."

April was frustrated. "I hate this place."

"Food getting to you?" He smiled.

"This entire place is getting to me."

He patted her arm. "Not much longer." He looked at Janice. "I have her old records from when she was five and I've gone over them. Unfortunately, the doctor who treated her then is deceased."

"Dr. Rubin was a good doctor. He operated, drained the tumor, and said he thought she'd be fine." Her mother's voice sounded challenging, as if daring Dr. Sorenson to contradict the other doctor's diagnosis.

"Yes, April had a low-grade astrocytoma."

April hated their talking around her, as if

she were still five years old. She remembered the nightmare of that time all too well. She hadn't understood what was happening to her, but she'd never forget the terror from the shots and IVs and being separated from her parents during the X-rays and surgery and recovery in ICU. But she'd recovered fully and up until now had led a perfectly normal life with a perfectly uncomplicated future.

"The headaches aren't the same," she told the doctor and her mother. "Before, when I was little, I mostly got dizzy and fell down a lot."

"She had a seizure," her mother confirmed. "We rushed her to the emergency room. But this time it seems different."

"No use speculating," Dr. Sorenson said. "We'll have some answers soon enough."

He left and April again thought about Mark. It was easier to think about him and his disease than it was to think about her own problems.

Eventually, her session in radiology was complete and she returned to her room. By now it was late afternoon and pale spring sunlight slanted through the window. Her father was waiting when they arrived. "How's my girl?"

She hugged him. "Bored. I didn't expect you here so early."

"I couldn't concentrate at the office, so I came over." He kissed his wife.

April saw the look that passed between them: *"Any news?"* her father's gaze asked. *"Nothing yet,"* her mother's eyes answered.

"Did you bring me these flowers?" April asked, wanting to distract them.

"I brought those." He pointed to a huge spring bouquet of irises, jonquils, and sweetheart roses. "I don't know who sent the other."

The other was a single red rose in a blue bud vase.

"It has a card." Her mother handed her a small envelope.

April opened it and read: *You're beautiful. Mark.*

"A secret admirer?" Her father craned his neck to see the signature. "I'm jealous."

April quickly shoved the card back inside the envelope. "No need to be. I'm still yours."

He laughed and looped his arm around his wife's waist. This was the way April was used to seeing them. None of her friends' parents acted as much in love as hers did. When her friends complained about parents who argued and threatened divorce, April could only listen, glad that her parents' relationship was so totally different.

"When this is over," her father said, "when they release you to go home, why don't we think about going to Spain again? We had such a good time there last summer."

"Oh, Hugh, let's!" her mother said. "Caroline won't miss me at the store. I'll tell her I'll pick up some special pieces. We actually had a customer come in looking for some fifteenth-century Spanish chairs the other day."

"Excuse me," April said, holding up her hand to stop their plan before her father rushed out and bought the tickets. "But I still have this small matter of finishing my senior year."

"You could miss a couple of weeks," her father declared.

April smiled indulgently. "Sorry, I don't want to go. I've spent twelve years slogging through classes so that I could enjoy being a senior. Kelli and I have a big countdown calendar on the inside of my locker where we're marking off each day till graduation. So count me out of your impromptu trip."

"We can't go without you." Her mother looked thoughtful. "Maybe we could think about going right after graduation."

"It could be your graduation present," her father added.

April wanted to spend the summer with her friends and Chris, and plan for their beach trip. But she decided not to make an issue of it just yet. The rattle of the dinner cart coming down the hall interrupted the conversation. "Are you two going down to the cafeteria?" April asked.

Her mother wrinkled her nose and her father shook his head vigorously. "I've made other arrangements."

"Such as?" her mother asked.

He grinned impishly. "How does The Red Dragon sound?" That was their favorite restaurant—and one of New York's most trendy. "Don't worry," he added quickly, "I've gotten special permission from the hospital. Turns out that the chief administrator is one of my clients. What could he say when I asked?

I mean, he still wants his investments to earn for him, doesn't he?"

"Daddy!" April squealed. "That's criminal."

"No . . . what they pass off as food here is criminal."

Within the hour, two waiters rolled a small cart into April's room, complete with a bright red linen tablecloth and napkins, candles, and succulent-smelling platters of Chinese food. April heard the commotion in the hall as the cart neared her room and she wondered what the other patients and the staff must be thinking. And she wondered what Mark might be thinking too.

She put some classical music on her portable CD player. Her mother made a special arrangement of flowers from those she'd received, and her father turned off all the lights. The three of them ate by candlelight. April listened to her mother describe various oddball customers and her father talk about a client who was also a rock star. And she almost forgot where she was and why she was there.

At the end of the meal, they each opened a fortune cookie. Laughing, they read the strips of paper aloud. April's mother was informed that she would be showered with riches; her father that he was wise and admired.

April pulled out the fortune tucked inside her cookie and a small shiver crept through her as she read the words on the paper. It read: *A change is coming. Be prepared.*

4

April was alone in her room the following day when Mark knocked on her door. "You up for a visit?"

"Sure." April closed the book she was reading. "How are you doing?"

"I may get out tomorrow if I pass all my breath tests." She must have looked puzzled because he explained, "There's a machine I have to blow air into and the gauge has to jump into a certain zone. That lets my doctor know how much lung capacity I've regained."

"I hope you pass."

"How about you?" he asked. "Know anything more about your problems?"

"Not yet. I'm not too sure I want to know

either. I mean, as long as I don't know, I can pretend it's nothing really bad."

"Why do you think it might be bad? You look healthy. I'll bet you've never been sick a day in your life."

"You're wrong." April wanted—*needed*— to confide her fears to somebody. On impulse she decided to tell Mark about her childhood brain tumor. "I've got plenty of reason to be worried," she said, and told him her story.

Mark listened intently, nodding and looking grim. "It must have been horrible for you."

"It was. But why am I telling you? You're certainly no stranger to hospitals."

"I honestly can't remember my life without them. CF and I reluctantly share the same body. Unless medical science comes up with a miracle, it's here to stay."

"I don't know how you stand it."

"I consider the alternative," he said with a wry smile.

April sighed. "I guess you're right. The alternative is what you're trying so hard to avoid."

"So let me get this straight," he said, moving back to their original topic. "After years of feeling fine, you suddenly start getting headaches and dizzy spells again."

"I staggered around like I was drunk. And I blacked out too."

"So you're afraid the tumor is back, even though they told you twelve years ago it was gone?"

"Yes, I am."

He looked at her and for a minute nothing existed except the dark brown of his eyes. "I hope you're wrong," he said softly. "I can't imagine anything terrible happening to you."

April suddenly felt self-conscious. She struggled to find something else to talk about. Her gaze fell on the bud vase. "Thank you for the rose. It was nice of you."

"It looks pretty puny next to your other bouquet."

"My dad never does anything halfway."

"You're lucky he can afford to do things first class." He paused. "April, when this is over, when you're out of here, can I call you? Come see you?"

April hesitated. His interest in her was flattering, but she couldn't lead him on. "No, Mark. I told you I have a boyfriend." His expression told her that he didn't think this was a good reason. "I mean it, Mark. Once I get out of here and back to my real life, I don't want any reminders of this place."

"Including me?"

"You've been nice to me and I appreciate it. But this is only a temporary interruption of my life."

"No matter what your tests say?"

She squared her chin. "No matter what the tests say."

Her parents were with her when Dr. Sorenson came in, pulled up a chair, and said, "I believe we have a diagnosis."

April's mouth went dry and her heart began to hammer. Her parents were on either side of her bed. They reminded her of guard dogs jealously surrounding their young. "May I have the envelope, please?" she said, trying hard to keep things light.

"You *are* having a recurrence of your earlier problem," Dr. Sorenson told them matter-of-factly.

"But they told us it was gone," April's mother said fiercely.

"They told you it was a *low-grade* astrocytoma and that the chances were good that it would not return," Dr. Sorenson corrected her. "But it's never been gone; it's only been dormant."

April suddenly felt cold, as if all her blood had turned to ice. She clenched her teeth to keep them from chattering.

"So what is it now?" April's father growled impatiently.

"Now it's a *high-grade* astrocytoma."

"Meaning?"

"It's growing rapidly and consequently it will be harder to treat."

"This is ridiculous," her father snapped. "First it's there, then it's gone, now it's back. Can't you doctors get it right? This is my daughter we're discussing."

"I'm very sorry," Dr. Sorenson said. "I wish I had better news for you."

Her father rocked back on his heels. "What are our options?"

April scarcely heard him. A rushing sound was filling up her ears and their voices seemed to be coming from far away. This couldn't be happening. It had to be some mistake.

Dr. Sorenson attached X rays to a portable light board he'd brought into the room with him. A human skull was outlined perfectly. "This is your skull, April. And here"—he pointed to a dark area at the base of her skull—"is the tumor. You can see it better on the MRI." They peered at the contours of her brain on another piece of film. The tumor looked dense and sinister. "The tumor's entrenched here, and it's growing."

April shuddered. How could something be growing inside her body without her knowledge or permission? "Can't you cut it out, remove it?" she asked.

"Maybe not."

"Why not?" asked her mother.

"It's embedded itself in the cerebellum here, near the brain stem." Dr. Sorenson pointed to the area on the MRI. "This is the part of your brain that's responsible for involuntary reflexes, like breathing and coordination. That explains your dizzy spells. The tumor mass is pressing and intruding into these areas. If we do traditional surgery, you could be maimed for life. No scalpel can untangle it."

"Are you saying there's nothing you can do?" April's mother gasped, her eyes wide with fear.

"No. We're going to try some things. First, a drug to reduce brain swelling. There are some side effects, but I want to get the swelling down so that you won't have so much pain."

"What kind of side effects?" April swallowed hard, feeling slightly detached, as if they were discussing someone else.

"Water retention, puffiness, and an incredible appetite."

April had always been tall and slim and able to eat whatever she wanted, and she didn't like the idea of a forced weight gain. "I'll look like a freak."

"What else?" her father asked the doctor.

"We'll start her on radiation treatments."

April remembered the radiation sessions from before. They had strapped her on a table, alone in a room, with a massive machine aimed at the back of her head. She'd shrieked and screamed, not because it hurt—it hadn't—but because she couldn't move. And because she was all alone. But she was older now and she knew that the technician had to leave the room to avoid the high doses of gamma rays emitted by the machine. Still, just the memory terrified her. "Will I lose my hair?" she asked. "Will I have to cut it off?"

"Just a little spot in the back. You can comb the rest of it over. No one will be able to tell. Radiation has come a long way. You'll have a radiation oncologist, a special doctor who does only these treatments. It's an exacting science and you'll be in good hands."

"But she's already had radiation once," April's mother interjected.

"It's the best treatment for this kind of tumor," the doctor insisted. "We must radiate again."

"And once it's shrunk?" her mother wanted to know.

"Then more MRIs and X rays to see if she's a candidate for gamma knife surgery."

"I thought you said you couldn't cut out the tumor."

"Not with a regular scalpel, but with a gamma knife, a high concentration of gamma rays aimed at the tumor."

"Why can't you just do that right away?" April asked breathlessly. "Why do I have to go through all the other stuff first?"

"Because we can't use the gamma knife on

anything larger than three centimeters." He pulled a ruler from his pocket and held his thumb on a mark. "Right now, your tumor is larger, about five centimeters."

She watched his thumb slide upward on the ruler and wondered how two centimeters could make such a difference. And yet it did. Surgery was out.

"What about chemotherapy?" her mother asked. "I have a friend who had breast cancer and they gave her chemo. She was sick for a while, but it worked. She's been cancer-free for six years."

Dr. Sorenson shook his head. "Chemo is ineffective on this kind of tumor."

April felt as if the doors of her options were being closed. "I don't have a lot of choices, do I?"

"Radiation's your best hope," the doctor answered.

She felt sick to her stomach. "And if radiation doesn't work?" Her voice trembled, but she *had* to ask the question.

"We'll cross that bridge when we come to it," he said.

But she knew instinctively that the bridge was a narrow rope hanging over a precipice that led down to a dark abyss. She turned her face into her mother's shoulder and hid, like a frightened child.

"You're leaving?"

Mark stood in April's doorway, and she turned at the sound of his voice.

"Mom's downstairs finishing up my paperwork now." April continued to pack her small valise.

He came up beside her. "I'm getting out today too."

"Oh, Mark, that's good. I'm glad for you."

"I'm sorry your news wasn't better."

"I guess I'm not destined to be normal and healthy after all."

"When do you start your radiation?"

She should have been surprised that he knew so much about her case, but she knew that the hospital floor was a hotbed of gossip. "Next week. Five days a week for six weeks. So, I guess I can kiss my extracurricular activities goodbye."

"I brought you a present," he said. From behind his back he pulled a large red balloon with a hand-drawn smiley face on it and tied with a long yellow ribbon. "I blew it up myself . . . which is what I used to do when I was a kid to prove I was well enough to get out of the hospital and go home."

The gift touched her. "Thank you."

Their hands brushed as she took the ribbon from him. Her skin tingled from the contact.

"Take care of yourself."

"I will."

"Uh—my phone number is written on a scrap of paper inside the balloon." A wide grin lit up his face. Then, more soberly, he continued, "Just in case you ever want to talk. Sometimes talking helps. And I'm a good listener."

"I told you—"

"I know, you have a boyfriend. But if things change between you two, call me."

She held on to the bright yellow ribbon and watched him walk from the room.

5

"A brain tumor! Oh, April, I can't believe it," Kelli gasped.

Seeing her friend so upset made April want to cry. But she quickly took hold of Kelli's hands. "I'll be okay," she said without much conviction. "Some radiation, some pills, and it'll shrink enough so the doctors can operate."

Kelli had come over the afternoon she'd returned from the ski trip. The two of them were sitting on the bedroom floor on plush pale lavender carpet. April's entire room was decorated in rich shades of purple accented with pure white. The down comforter on her four-poster bed was covered in white eyelet, and plum-colored pillows rested against the pristine whiteness. Without the drabness of the hospital surrounding her, April's diagnosis seemed like a bad dream.

"It's not fair!" Kelli blurted out. "You've never done anything mean to anybody. Why should *you* get sick?"

"What's being mean got to do with anything?"

"Well, there are tons of bad people in the world. They're the ones who should get brain tumors." Kelli sounded furious.

"I guess life doesn't work that way. I'm proof that bad things can happen to anybody."

"Have you told Chris?" Kelli asked.

"I'll tell him tonight. We're supposed to go out to dinner." April hugged her knees. "I'm dreading it."

"Why?"

"I'm not sure how he'll handle it."

"He'll be mad about it—like me."

But Chris wasn't like Kelli. Kelli was her best friend. April and Chris had only been together a few months, and they weren't nearly as close as she and Kelli. How *would* Chris react? "I just don't know," she said, chewing on her bottom lip.

Kelli blew her nose. "This is just the worst thing to ever happen."

"Listen, do me a favor."

"Anything."

"I don't want this to get all around school. It's nobody's business but mine."

"But everyone knew you couldn't go on the ski trip because you were in the hospital. They'll want to know what the doctors told you."

"If anyone asks you, tell them I'm being treated for migraine headaches or something. I don't want them to know about the tumor."

"But why?"

"I don't want kids whispering about me in the halls and treating me like I'm contagious or something."

"But that's dumb. Everybody knows you can't catch a brain tumor like you can a cold." Kelli paused. "Can you?"

For a moment, April couldn't tell if Kelli was joking, but then a sly grin broke across Kelli's face. "Just a little humor," she said.

April nodded sheepishly. She was tired of thinking about what was happening to her. Tired of feeling sorry for herself and for her parents, who had been in despair ever since she'd come home from the hospital. She wanted her life back to normal. She wanted to get on with the radiation treatments and get them over with and have her life the way it used to be. "So, let's talk about something else," she said crisply. "How was the ski trip?"

"All right. Not nearly as much fun as if you'd been there."

"That's nice of you to say."

"It's true."

"Well, I *am* going to the shore with everybody this summer. It'll be our last blowout and I'm not about to miss it."

An awkward silence fell between them. The summer seemed so far away. How could they make plans when no one knew if April would be well?

"What's that?" Kelli broke the silence. She pointed to the limp balloon tied to the doorknob of April's bathroom.

April told her about meeting Mark.

"I remember that he was cute, but gee . . . his being sick—it's kind of a turnoff."

" 'A turnoff'?"

"I didn't mean it the way it sounded," Kelli insisted. "You're not him."

"That's exactly why I don't want kids to know about me," April said emphatically. "It's *all* a big turnoff."

Kelli hung her head and then mumbled, "Sorry."

Already April could feel the gap opening between them. Kelli belonged to the world of perfect health, while she belonged . . . ? Where? Suddenly she didn't know either. She thought of Mark and wondered how he managed to straddle the two worlds of sickness and health. How could she find a place for herself in this new world where all the rules had changed?

Chris picked her up that night and took her to the country club where most people in their Long Island community had memberships. Normally, April didn't mind going there, but tonight she didn't want the quiet country club atmosphere. She felt like loud music and pizza and having to shout above the noise. Maybe because that way Chris might not really hear her when she told him about her tumor. In the quiet elegance of the country club, there would be no mistaking her words.

"You look great," Chris said, taking her hand across the table. "And I missed you like crazy."

"I'll bet you didn't even have time to think about me. What with the tournament and all. How did your team do?"

His face clouded. "We came in second. We should have won, but Andy got a red card and we had to play a man down the whole second half of the final game."

"Bummer."

He grinned and April couldn't help noticing how different his smile was from Mark's. Chris's eyes didn't light up in the same way as Mark's. "But I want to hear about you. What did those doctors say?"

Her heart began to hammer so loudly she was afraid that he might hear it on his side of the table. "Well . . . the news wasn't great."

"What do you mean?"

She forced a smile and said flippantly, "I have some wild and crazy cells growing in my brain. They've set up housekeeping and my doctor has to radiate them out of existence. Actually, it's a recurrence of a tumor that I had when I was five."

He stared at her, as if sorting out her answer. "You've got some kind of tumor? Inside your head?"

"So it seems."

He sagged back in his chair and stared at her. "Is this some kind of joke?"

Her face felt frozen. "No joke."

"I don't believe it."

"I wouldn't make it up."

"I don't know what to say."

Say anything, she thought.

"You had a tumor before?"

"When I was five."

"Why didn't you ever tell me?"

His question made her hesitate. She wasn't sure what she'd expected from him, but she recalled how Kelli had taken the news. And Mark. In so many words they both had said, "I'm here for you." Chris seemed almost angry at her.

She told Chris, "I thought it wouldn't ever be a problem for me again. My doctors told me it wouldn't, so I didn't see any reason to talk about it."

"You shouldn't hide things from people you care about." He sounded upset, accusatory.

"Would it have mattered?" April was feeling light-headed, but it had nothing to do with her medical condition.

"Of course not," he said a little too quickly. "It's just that you should have told me. I would have liked to know."

"I was only five. It wouldn't have made any difference." But the expression on Chris's face told her otherwise. "Would it?"

He quickly reached across the table and took her hand. "No. I—I just can't stand the thought of you being sick. I don't want you to be sick." He was picking through his words like a soldier inching through a field of land mines.

Chris was an athlete. In prime physical condition. Strong, muscular, and fit. To him, being sick must be a horror. "I hate what's happening to me, Chris." Tears swam in her eyes. She didn't want to cry, but she couldn't help herself.

He sprang from his chair, knelt beside her, and pulled her against his chest. "I'm sorry, April. Really sorry."

Everyone was sorry. She wept while he rocked her. As her tears slowed, she noticed other diners staring at her and Chris. Self-consciously, she pulled back and wiped her tears on the linen table napkin. "I didn't mean to lose it like that," she said hoarsely.

"You all better now?" Chris asked.

She wasn't all right. She never would be again. "Sure," she lied. "But I've lost my appetite."

"You want me to take you home?"

"Yes."

They left and Chris was silent during the ride home. It was just as well. April wasn't sure what else to say to him. At her front door, he took her in his arms again, but his touch was tentative, as if she'd suddenly been turned to glass and he had to be extra careful in handling her. "I wish this wasn't happening," he breathed into her hair.

"So do I."

He kissed her and she wanted to cling to him and not let go.

He cleared his throat. "I have a game Monday after school. Will you come cheer for me?"

"I can't. I have a consultation with the doctor who's doing my radiation. Then the treatments start." She explained the schedule.

"Every day!" He protested. "You'll miss my whole soccer season."

"I don't have a choice."

"So will you glow in the dark?"

He was attempting to be funny, but April wasn't in the mood to laugh. "No," she said. "But if I'm lucky, the tumor will shrink."

"Of course it will shrink."

She asked, "Do you want to come in? I could make you a sandwich since I made you miss dinner."

He shook his head. "I'm not hungry."

Chris quickly said goodnight. And as she watched him climb into his sports car, maneuver it around the wide brick circular driveway, and drive away, she felt cold and empty. She wrapped her coat closer around her and hurried inside the house.

6

Dr. Sorenson arranged for April to receive her radiation treatments at a Long Island hospital. She would still have to make the trek into the city to see Dr. Sorenson throughout her treatments, but at least she could be treated each day closer to home.

She tried to go to the hospital by herself Monday afternoon, but Janice Lancaster wouldn't hear of it. "I won't tag along for all your treatments," her mother assured her, "but I want to be there for the preliminaries."

April's radiation oncologist was Dr. Edith Hamilton, a short plump woman with graying hair who wore no makeup. She explained about the treatments thoroughly and then carefully shaved away a hank of April's thick red hair at the base of her skull. While studying April's X rays, she took a pen and mapped out the area that was to be bombarded with the gamma rays. Next, Dr. Hamilton used a small needle to make permanent dots in the skin at the base of April's skull. It didn't really hurt; it felt like tiny pinpricks. "Little tattoos," the doctor called the dots, "so that the technician can always align the machine precisely." Her hands were quick and felt like the fluttering wings of small birds in April's hair.

April's mother watched intently. "I thought this was all behind us," she said. "I feel as though we were lulled into a false sense of security."

"April's case is unusual," Dr. Hamilton answered. "This is rare—one in a thousand."

Why do I have to be the one? April thought. It was a question no one could answer. April straightened her hair, combing it over the bald spot at the back of her head. She still felt as if everyone could see the blue marks through the veil of hair. Her mother assured her that nothing showed.

"Be careful when you wash your hair," Dr. Hamilton said. "We'll re-mark the area from

time to time, but don't get soap on the skin."
April couldn't imagine how she was going to
wash her hair and not get soap on her skin.
The doctor continued. "You will lose some of
your hair, but because the treatment is so lo-
calized, I hope it won't be much. You may
experience dry mouth and food may lose some
of its taste, but don't let it keep you from
eating. Your skin will get red at the site, but
don't use any creams. Creams interfere with
the rays. Toward the end of treatment you
may experience fatigue. All these symptoms
will vanish once the treatment is completed."

"Can't I start today?" April asked.

"Tomorrow," Dr. Hamilton said. "But let
me show you the equipment we'll be using.
It's state of the art."

They went into a large room with a huge
machine. It sprouted a thick mechanical arm
with a cone-shaped device at one end. "We'll
point this at your skull, aim it at the tumor,
and zap the growth," Dr. Hamilton explained
as she touched the cone. "We'll take more
X-ray pictures periodically to track the tumor's
shrinkage."

April felt her hands growing clammy. Memories from when she was five years old and terrified flooded her mind. She told herself that her fear was irrational. "I'll be back tomorrow," she said, turning on her heel, eager to get away from the room and the machine.

School let out at three, so they set her appointments at four o'clock, the last time slot of the day. April went to bed that night and lay in the dark with her eyes open, trying not to cry, trying to grasp the monumental change that was occurring in her life. Just before she finally fell asleep, she realized that Chris hadn't called since their almost dinner date. She knew if it had been Chris going through this ordeal, she would have called.

The next day, at school, she could scarcely keep her mind on her classes. She saw Chris in the lunchroom and he came straight over to her. "How's it going?" he asked.

"I start treatments today at four," she said.

"You're okay with it, aren't you?"

"As okay as a person can be, I guess." She looked up at him. "Why didn't you call me last night?"

He looked away. "The game went into overtime. By the time I got home, showered, and ate, it was late. Then I had to work on a history paper. I tried to call once, but your line was busy."

She would never know if he was telling her the truth.

"I miss you cheering for me," he said.

And I miss you cheering for me, she thought, but she said, "See you in English class."

After school, she went to the hospital, signed in, and fidgeted in the waiting area until her name was called. With her heart pounding, she entered the treatment room, fighting a stomach filled with butterflies. A cheerful technician didn't make her feel any better, and when she lay on the table and heard the machine whirl into gear, she tensed. "Lie perfectly still," the tech said. "You'll hear a buzzing sound, then I'll reposition the machine via remote control, and you'll hear another buzzing sound. I'll be out of the room until it clicks off."

April heard the heavy metal door of the room close as the tech left, and she knew she was all alone. She was shaking. She bit her lip and held her breath, hoping it would stop the trembling.

The treatment was over in a few minutes and the tech returned with a smile. "You did fine." Then he added, "You look pale. Feel all right?"

"I'm okay," she said breathlessly.

"There's free juice in the waiting room. Why don't you grab some on your way out and get your blood sugar up a bit. You'll feel better."

She didn't want juice. She just wanted to leave. Out in the parking lot, she blinked against the brilliant spring sunlight. The air was cool and she slowly began to feel better. She glanced around, trying to remember where she'd parked her car, when she heard a horn honk and turned to see an aqua and white car with gleaming chrome coming toward her. Her mouth dropped as the car stopped in front of her and Mark Gianni grinned at her through the open window. "Want a ride? Hop in."

"I—I have my car . . . ," she sputtered.

"Not so," he said with his million-watt smile. "You have transportation. *This* is a car."

"What are you doing here?"

"When you didn't call me, I decided to come see you."

She'd tossed out the balloon he'd given her

days before, without ever retrieving the slip of paper containing his phone number from it. Now she felt guilty about it. "I had my first treatment," she said.

"I know." He leaned over and popped the passenger door handle. "Come on. Let's go get a soda."

She climbed into the car. The white leather seat felt smooth against the backs of her legs. Mark put the car in gear and drove out of the parking lot toward the small strip mall across the street. "I saw a coffee shop while I waited for you to come out. Is it okay?"

She nodded, still stunned at seeing him. She knew it was a long commute from the city and couldn't figure how he'd managed to track her down.

Inside the coffee shop they ordered cappuccino, and when it was served, she sipped it, waiting for him to explain himself.

"You look beautiful," he said.

"You came all this way to tell me that?"

"I came because I wanted to see you again. Because I *had* to see you again."

"But how—?"

"I can't reveal my sources. But I *did* find

out that your treatments began today and I *am* here to give you moral support. Plus," he added with a grin, "I wanted to be with you again. And since it seemed like you weren't ever going to call me, I decided to make the first move. Or, actually, the second move. So, here I am."

His forwardness made April a little uncomfortable, but she couldn't pretend that his presence didn't mean something to her. "You ever have radiation?" she asked, changing the subject.

"No. But I've had more than my share of medical treatments."

She knew it was true. And while her friends were sympathetic, Mark was *empathetic*—he knew firsthand what she was experiencing. "I thought I'd be able to handle it better than I did," she said. She told him of her fears, and once the words started coming, she couldn't stop them. She told him how she felt alienated from friends and smothered by her parents. She told him things she hadn't even realized she'd been feeling until they spilled out of her. He listened intently, never taking his gaze off her face, and when she was finished, and her eyes had filled with tears, he took a paper napkin and dabbed her cheeks tenderly.

"That's sure a lot of baggage you've been carrying around."

She blew her nose and nodded. "Thanks for letting me dump it on you."

"No thanks necessary. We're comrades in medical misery."

"How have you done it all these years?"

"I keep hoping there will be some big breakthrough, some kind of medical miracle. There's been some progress lately. A new medication. Lung transplants. But nothing that's right for me just yet. So I keep on waiting. And I try to live as normal a life as possible. Because while you have to respect your disease, you can't let it control you. If you do, it robs you of what's good about life." He reached across the table and took her hand. "And there's a lot of good in life."

She felt her heart skip a beat. "Are you flirting with me again?"

"Absolutely."

She smiled, and this time she didn't push him away. "I still have that boyfriend."

"How is Mr. Lucky anyway?"

"Mr. Lucky? You mean Chris?"

"Is that the guy I saw you with at the hospital?"

"Yes." She pulled her hand away. "He's struggling with all this. I understand. But still . . ."

"His loss," Mark said, his smile lighting up his eyes. "My gain."

"But we haven't broken up," she told Mark.

"No problem. All I want is a chance with you. All I want is for you to go out with me, just once, and get to know me. After that, if you tell me to get lost, I'll do it."

"That would be pretty cold."

"Believe me, it's happened."

For a moment she saw through his cheerful smile and into the hurt of rejection beneath it. Ashamed, she recalled that avoiding him had been her first reaction also. "Well, whoever told you to get lost wasn't much of a catch," she said. Then she took a deep breath and added, "If you want to call me, it's all right. If you ask me out, I'll go. Once."

He raised his fist in the air and said, "Yes!"

She laughed. "I'm not that big a deal."

"Yes you are," he said with a grin. "To me, you're a really big deal."

April smiled. For the first time in days, she was looking forward to something.

7

"You told Mark you'd go out with him?" Kelli sounded incredulous.

April sorted through her locker. "What's wrong with that?"

"Well, what about Chris?"

"I don't think I'm at the top of Chris's list anymore."

"Why do you think that?"

"Ever since he found out about my tumor, he's backed off. He hasn't called once since I broke the news to him."

"Maybe he's just going through an adjustment period."

April rolled her eyes. "*You* didn't go through one." She found her literature book and heaved it into her backpack.

"But I'm your best friend."

"And what was Chris? Wasn't he supposed to be my 'best' guy?"

Kelli shrugged. "What makes Mark so special? You weren't interested in him at all before now."

"Mark accepts me." April slammed her locker door. "The way I am."

"You mean he isn't put off by your tumor."

Kelli was right. But April knew it was more than that. There was something special about Mark she couldn't explain. "The next six weeks aren't going to be a picnic," she said, feeling overwhelmed by what lay ahead of her. "Mark seems to understand, without any explanation. He knows because he's been through it too."

"Except that there's one big difference," Kelli said before April could rush off.

"And what's that?"

"You're going to get well. Mark isn't."

April walked away without answering.

By the end of the first week of radiation treatments, April was ready for a change. She was tired of her life revolving around cancer, so when Mark came to pick her up Saturday morning, she was eager to go. Her parents weren't thrilled—they thought he was too old for her—but Mark was charming and pleasant. By the time she and Mark left the house, April thought her parents were somewhat pacified.

Sunshine gleamed through the windshield of Mark's car as they drove toward the city. Blooming wildflowers grew along the sides of the road like bright punctuation marks of color. "So what are we doing today?" April asked.

"I'm introducing you to my world. I've seen yours—lifestyles of the rich and famous—so I thought I'd show you mine."

"You exaggerate."

"I've just been inside your family mansion, so I think I know what I'm talking about."

His tone was friendly, but it hadn't really occurred to April that their material worlds were so very different. "So what part of your world do you want me to see?"

"All of it. Where I work, where I live. Oh, and did I mention, my mother is expecting us for dinner?"

"No, you didn't mention it." She wasn't sure how she felt about being thrust into his family life so soon. She'd barely gotten to know him.

He must have sensed her reluctance because he hastily added, "I told you . . . we're a close family. Mom's a great cook. Her dinners could feed a small country."

"I'll meet your family, but I don't know what they're expecting."

"An angel," he said.

"Then they're in for a rude awakening," she countered.

Mark drove to Brooklyn and he parked his car inside a building that was both a garage and a workshop. It was littered with auto parts and the partial shells of car bodies. "We're restoring a fifty-six Thunderbird now," he said proudly, showing April around. He patted a car that needed a paint job. "And this old Dodge may not look like much, but it has a muscle engine. It's our best racing machine."

She thought the place felt cold and looked dingy. It smelled of motor oil and grease, but Mark was obviously proud of it. She stopped beside the Thunderbird. "Will you sell it or race it when you're finished?"

"Sell it. Maybe I'll build one for you some-day. Any preferences?"

She didn't want to admit she didn't know one car from another, so she said, "Surprise me."

Out on the sidewalk he said, "We don't have to be at my parents' place until five."

"All right," she told him. "I glimpsed your world, now I want you to come do something with me in mine."

"Such as?"

"How about lunch at Trump Plaza?"

They took a cab because it was easier than driving through the city. Once inside the op-ulent glass and marble plaza, April felt more comfortable. She chose a quiet restaurant with booths and crisp linen tablecloths, a place where she'd often eaten with her mother.

Mark studied the menu, which was in French. "You know French?"

"Oui." She giggled because he looked im-pressed.

"You've been to France?"

"We went when I was thirteen."

"I've never been out of New York."

"I won't hold it against you."

He put down the menu. "How do you order bread and water?"

"How about onion soup and a salad?" He agreed and when the waiter came, she ordered—in English.

"Cute," he told her, but he smiled because she'd so smoothly taken him in.

Afterward, she dragged him through a few of the trendier stores in the plaza. Mark kept doing double takes at the price tags. He made her laugh, and much later she realized he had made her forget what was really happening in her life.

Late in the afternoon they caught a cab downtown to Little Italy. "My folks have lived here all their lives," Mark told her. When the cab pulled up in front of an old brownstone, Mark paid the driver and, taking April's hand, led her up the front steps. "Pop brought Mom here right after they got married."

Once inside, April smelled rich tomato sauce, garlic, and onions. In a room off the front hallway, a giant-screen television was blaring a basketball game and a man was yelling at the televised image. He sprang to his feet when Mark and April entered the room. "Dad, this is April," Mark said.

He held out his hand and April clasped it. "Been looking forward to this." He pumped her arm vigorously. "Hey, ladies," he yelled. "They're here."

From another room three women emerged, one older with graying hair, wiping her hands on an apron. They hovered around Mark and April, all talking at once, all hugging one another. April learned that the older woman was Rosa, Mark's mother. The others were his sisters, Marnie and Jill. Mark's mother took both of April's hands and beamed her a smile. "Let me get a good look at you. Oh, Mark, you didn't lie. She's beautiful."

April felt her cheeks flame and cast Mark a sidelong look. "Don't smother her," he said with a laugh. "And don't scare her off." He slid his arm around April's waist. "She's not used to being pounced on, you know."

April joined in the laughter with the others, although she felt a bit overwhelmed by his family. "What exactly did you tell them about me?" she whispered to him as Mark's mother led them all to the dining room table.

"Nothing," he insisted innocently.

She sat beside Mark and watched him take

his medication. Her mouth felt parched and she took a sip of water. She wondered if this was a side effect of her radiation.

Platters of food were passed and conversation flowed like water. It was different from meals at her house, but it was fun listening to them talk and joke with one another. She answered questions politely and wondered how much they knew about her, how much Mark might have told them.

"So, Mark," Marnie asked. "You racing next weekend?"

Instantly, April felt tension close around the table like a fist.

"Yeah," he said nonchalantly. "I'm running the Dodge."

"Why?" his mother asked bluntly. "You know it's not good for you."

"Ma, please." He gave her a look and then cut his eyes toward April. "I have a guest. Let's not argue."

"It makes me crazy," his mother insisted, ignoring Mark's plea. "You shouldn't be breathing in all those fumes."

"Ma, please—"

"Leave the kid alone, Rosa," Mark's father said.

"You know you don't approve," Rosa told him. "Why pretend in front of company?"

"Who's pretending? All I'm saying is now isn't the time to bring this up."

"And when should I? When he's in the hospital?"

April felt caught in the cross fire.

Mark pushed back from the table. "Ma, we got to go."

"I just want you to think about the consequences," his mother declared. "Please, Mark, you're barely out of the hospital. Why tempt fate?"

But Mark ignored her and headed for the front door. "I'm out of here," he called over his shoulder.

April hastily wadded her napkin and stood. "Um-m-m . . . thanks for the dinner. It was delicious."

"And thank you for coming," Mark's father said, standing. "Sorry things kind of deteriorated."

"Yes, sorry," Rosa said. "You're a lovely girl. You take good care of my Mark. And try and talk some sense into him. Maybe he'll listen to you."

April bolted from the room, through the front door, and down the steps. She saw Mark halfway up the street. "Wait!" she called.

He stopped and when she caught up with him, she was angry. "What do you think you're doing? Were you going to leave me there?"

He looked miserable. "I just had to get away. I go nuts when they start in on me about my racing."

"Well, they have a point, you know. You have a disease that seriously affects your breathing. Not to mention that speeding cars can be hazardous to your health in general." She was mad. Mad at the way a perfectly fine day had soured. Mad at the way Mark was acting. Mad at herself for caring about what happened to him.

He grabbed her by the shoulders, his eyes fierce with determination. "But it's *my* life!" he exclaimed. "It belongs to *me*, Mark Gianni. You of all people should understand that."

And suddenly, she did understand it. Racing cars was something he could control. Cystic fibrosis was something he couldn't. And neither was brain cancer. Tears filled her eyes.

Mark pulled her to him, crushing her against his chest. He put his finger beneath her chin and tilted her face upward. Their lips met and he kissed her longingly. "I'm sorry, April. I'm sorry. Please give me another chance."

8

The feel of Mark's lips against hers left April breathless. His impassioned plea shocked her. She hadn't anticipated feeling such a strong emotional reaction to him, and she stepped away. "I'm not going to desert you just because you ran off and left me stranded with your parents."

He looked shaken but relieved. "I didn't mean to leave you alone in there, but I had no idea Mom was going to get on her soapbox in front of you. I thought she knew better than to embarrass me like that."

"Parents don't need excuses," April told him. "I think hospitals give out instruction books on 'how to embarrass your kid' when they send parents home with their babies.

Then, no matter what your age, they open the book and drag out some gem, use it in front of your friends, and make you wish you could fade into the floor."

He grinned. "Your parents have done this to you too?"

"I could write a book, but why bother? They'd only embarrass me with it."

His grin broadened. "Thanks for understanding. Sorry if your dinner got ruined."

"It's okay. Who needs the calories?"

He brushed his hand along her cheek, causing a tingle to shoot up her spine. "I've never had a girl like you in my life before. I don't want you to go away."

They started walking along the sidewalk, and he led her into a small café. They sat at a table in the back and ordered two cappuccinos. They didn't speak right away, but stared out the window at the gathering gloom of the evening and at the lights coming on across the street. When the cappuccinos came, he stirred his, stopped, and reached across the table to take her hand. He held it lightly, rubbing his thumb across her knuckles. "If you're right about parents getting 'embarrassment' handbooks, then girls must get 'cruelty' ones."

"How can you say that? It isn't true." She attempted to pull her hand away, but he wouldn't let go.

"Hear me out. Please."

She nodded. "I'm listening."

"I've always been sick, April. I was born with CF, I grew up with CF. I will die with CF." She shuddered but didn't interrupt. "When a person's sick, especially with a disease that's never going to go away, he learns some tough lessons. He learns that other kids always treat him differently. Sometimes they even call him names, make fun of him."

"You were teased because you had CF?" She couldn't imagine it.

"Yeah. Kids can be that way, you know. If they don't understand, if they're afraid, they shun you. Not everybody . . . but most. Grade school was really rough. I was in and out of the hospital so much and I coughed and smelled like medicine. I couldn't play sports, and I was skinny, and nobody wanted to be my friend."

She wondered if she'd ever treated anybody that way, then remembered her first reaction to Mark. She hadn't even wanted to get to know him because *if he was in the hospital, he must be sick*. She sat very still, hoping she wouldn't have to confess she'd felt that way.

"Do you know what the cruelest thing is about being different?" he asked.

She shook her head.

"While your body is all tied up with sickness, your mind and feelings aren't. You still want all the same things that 'regular' people have. You still want to be liked. You still want friends and to be invited to places and, when you're older, to ask a girl out and not have her act all embarrassed . . . or worse, horrified. All through high school I wanted to date. I wanted to kiss a girl. I wanted to have a girlfriend. Look at me: I'm twenty-one years old and I've never heard a girl tell me 'I love you.' "

She didn't know what to say. His pain was real.

"There were times when I realized that I could *live* with my CF—if only I didn't have to *live* with my feelings. Why couldn't CF have taken my emotions away, instead of my breath?"

"I'm sorry for every mean word that was said to you," April told him. "I'm sorry for every girl who hurt you and rejected you."

He shrugged sheepishly. "This isn't a pity party. Honest. The *last* thing I want is for you to feel sorry for me, April. I can't help the way I feel about you. I wanted to date you the first time I laid eyes on you. But I also knew that getting a girl like you to date me was a longshot. So everything we've done together so far is beyond my expectations."

She felt her face grow warm. She hadn't encouraged him, and now she felt bad about it.

"I knew I was taking a chance at your blowing me off, but I had to try. I wanted to see you as much as you'd let me. Being with you today has been terrific."

His honesty unnerved her. She'd dated Chris for four months and he'd never once been so open with her about his thoughts and feelings. Looking at Mark, seeing his vulnerability in his eyes, twisted her insides. How could anyone have treated him cruelly? How could *she*?

"I do know what it's like to be sick, Mark. I didn't have to live with it like you did, but I have to live with it now. Believe me, it isn't any easier when it happens to you after you've grown up some and had a 'normal' life. I've been afraid of my friends finding out. Only a couple know." Her gaze fell to the coffee in her cup, which looked cold and unappetizing. She felt Mark squeeze her hand and she lifted her gaze and saw his face, compassionate and tender. A lump lodged in her throat. She didn't want to bawl. "My boyfriend," she said, "can't deal with what's happening to me. He's backed off so far, I'd have to fax him to get a message to him."

Mark chuckled. "His loss."

"But it's my problem." She toyed with the ends of her long red hair. "The doctor marked me up with a blue pen and every day I go into this room and they shut the door and shoot me full of radiation. Not very romantic, is it?"

"They only zap the tumor," he said.

"So what? I'm . . . different now. And as you know, different isn't always appreciated."

Mark's grip on her hand tightened. "If you will let me, I'll do everything possible to make you happy again."

"Happy." She said the word without emotion. "It's been so long since I've felt happy, I don't remember what it feels like."

"Let me try. All I want is a chance, April. Is that too much to ask?"

She didn't answer him, because she couldn't. His health was even more fragile than hers. How could she tell him she was frightened of taking a chance?

She resumed radiation treatments on Monday, resigning herself to another week of balancing her life between her regular high-school grind and medical necessity. She had stopped all her after-school activities and, except for Kelli, steered clear of most of her friends. She knew they knew about her problem. There was no way it could be kept a secret, but at least no one bugged her about it, or asked stupid questions like "How are you feeling?" or "Does it hurt?" She was positive that it was Kelli who kept everyone off her back, and she was grateful to her friend.

Mark called her nightly and they talked for hours. One night he told her, "I'm racing this Saturday night. Will you come watch?"

She was hesitant but curious about his passion for racing cars.

"My dad will be there," Mark said. "He's always been my biggest fan. You can sit with him and I'll get you a pass so you can come onto the infield."

April knew that saying yes would mean a shift in their relationship. "If I come, will you win?"

"If you come, I've already won."

She took a deep breath and agreed to go.

On Friday afternoon, as she was leaving school, she ran into Chris in the parking lot. He had his arm around a pretty junior named Hallie, but lowered it when he saw April. She turned on her brightest smile. "How's it going?"

"Fine," he said. "How are things with you?"

Hallie shifted awkwardly, looking as if she'd been caught doing something naughty.

"Couldn't be better."

"That's good."

"I hear you're leading the soccer team to all kinds of wins."

"I'm having a good season."

"And the rumor about you getting an athletic scholarship to Virginia, is that true?"

"It's been offered. I'll probably take it. It's a full ride."

April felt a twinge of jealousy that he was able to make college plans. "I know you'll do well wherever you go."

"And you? You pick a college yet?"

"Not yet," she said smoothly. "Sometimes a person's plans are forced to change."

For an instant, sadness filled his eyes, and . . . hurt? "I'm sorry."

And she saw that he meant it. "Don't worry about it. I'm going to make it through this, and my friends will help me."

His cheeks colored and she knew she'd made her point—he hadn't been much of a friend to her. But there was no way to let him know that in the long run, his abandonment had been the best thing for her. Otherwise she would not have made room for Mark. She slipped the key into the lock of her car door, knowing that if she didn't hurry, she'd be late for radiation. "Got to run," she called, pulling open the door. "Have a good life, Chris."

As she drove off, she saw Chris and Hallie in her rearview mirror. Their arms were linked around each other's waist. April wanted to feel something—remorse, anger, sadness. She and Chris were history. And she felt nothing at all.

9

❧❧❧❧

"Is it always so loud?" April shouted, not certain Mark could hear her over the roar of engine noise from cars warming up around the speedway track. Nighttime blanketed the sky, and artificial lights obscured the stars.

"It's beautiful music," Mark shouted back with a grin. "Come on." He led her around the exterior of the half-mile track and inside the inner field where cars were parked, surrounded by men in jeans and overalls, most smudged with grease and oil. "The crews are car fanatics," he said. "Each pit has a few people who help out. Drivers are usually the cars' owners. No one gets paid."

"You do this for free?"

"For bragging rights and some prize

money. We're pretty small-time, just a group of local car lovers. Of course, the really big races are driven by professionals on two- or three-mile tracks. I'll take you to one sometime."

April smiled. Mark seemed so excited by the whole business. His brown eyes fairly danced and he looked animated and energized. "How long do you race? Is it year-round?"

"Our season is from May until the snow flies. Tonight's for running cars in my car's class. Other nights, other kinds of cars run: dragsters, which are supermodified cars—the 'funny' ones, are over there on the straight track and the late-model stocks here on the oval. This is my first race this year, but I've got a good car and I expect to kick some butt tonight."

April met several of Mark's racing friends. She could barely hear their names above the din of the motors. Mark's car was a Chevelle, unpainted except for a coat of rust-colored primer. The hood was up and she saw a massive engine laced with wires and hoses. The smell of gasoline and exhaust made her eyes water and she wondered how Mark was able to breathe when even she was having trouble.

"How do you manage not to go deaf?" she shouted.

"These will help." He handed her a set of ear protectors that looked like the kind airplane mechanics wore. Putting them on muffled the noise considerably.

His father materialized from the side of the field. "You can sit with me," he yelled.

"I need a token," Mark told her as she started off with his dad.

"A token?"

"Something of yours to bring me luck."

"Gee, I don't know what I've got." She fumbled for some item and settled on the scarf she was wearing. It was an expensive one, given to her by her parents. "Is this okay?"

He grinned and wrapped it around his upper arm into a band, letting the tails flutter. He took her by the shoulders and planted a kiss on her mouth, shouting, "For *better* luck! See you in the winner's circle."

The noise wasn't as loud in the grandstands, which were already crowded with onlookers. "I didn't think so many people were into racing," she told Mark's father.

"It's a whole subculture. A lot of people love hot rods."

"Your wife didn't come?"

"Rosa's still mad because he's racing. It takes her half a season to get over it. Once she does, she comes. I like to come because it's good to see Mark doing something he loves and doing it well."

"Does he win a lot?"

"He's got bookcases full of trophies at his place. Didn't he show them to you?"

"Not yet."

"Well, he was never one to brag. And once a race is over, he forgets about it. He's looking ahead to the next one."

She could tell that Mark's father was proud of him but at the same time worried about him. "His mom's right, isn't she? Racing is hard on his CF."

"It isn't good for it. One whole season he wore a special mask around the track. But Rosa doesn't understand that the kid's got to have something to call his own. That his whole life can't revolve around CF—even though it does."

"I'm happy you support him," April said. "I know it means a lot to him."

He shrugged. "He's my son. I love him."

The racing began, and Mark's father ex-

plained that it was done in heats—the top fin-
ishers from each heat became the competitors
in the final race of the night. The winner of
the final heat would take home the prize
money and trophy. Mark would race in the
third of seven heats, and if he won that, he'd
run in the last. The cars were beginning to
accelerate around the track in anticipation of
the green go-ahead flag dropping and starting
their heat. April realized she was growing used
to the roar, so she slipped the hearing protectors partway off.

"This is it," she shouted when the cars
rolled out for the start of Mark's race. Mark's
primer-coated Chevelle looked intimidating
on the asphalt oval. She dug her nails into her
palms when the starter flag dropped and the
cars shot out of their slots, jockeying for posi-
tion. It didn't take Mark long to push his car
to the front of the pack. April let out a whoop
when he crossed under the checkered flag in
first place. "He made *that* look easy!" she exclaimed.

His father grinned proudly. "He usually
does."

For the rest of the evening, she fidgeted in
her seat, watching with keen interest the win-

ners of the following heats. By the final race she was squirming. "This is it," she declared as the winners of all the heats took to the track.

"Guess you're becoming a racing fan," Mark's father said with a wink.

"It's loud and smelly, but it's fun."

"True," he said. "And Mark loves it."

April held her breath as the green flag dropped and the cars roared forward. This time, Mark maneuvered quickly behind the lead car, hugging its back bumper. "What's he doing? Why doesn't he go around him?" she yelled.

"He's drafting," Mark's father explained above the whine of the engines. "He's letting the other car slice through the air to pull him along. It cuts down on his car's wind drag. Then, if it's timed just right and he can maneuver past him, the other driver can't do anything but eat his exhaust."

She watched, wide-eyed, as the cars rounded the final turn and roared down the stretch. At seemingly the last moment before the checkered flag dropped, Mark gunned his accelerator and flung his car around his opponent, crossing the finish line just a bumper ahead. The fans went wild. "He won!" April screamed, jumping up and down.

"Let's get to the winner's circle." Mark's father took her arm and pulled her down the steps and through an infield gate, where he showed his badge once more. In the winner's area, Mark's car stopped rolling. He switched off the motor and climbed out. Everyone applauded and she heard shouts of "Good driving!" and "Way to go!"

Mark tugged off his helmet, his smile brighter than the artificial lights over the field, and waved. But his gaze found April in the crowd instantly. She threw herself into his arms and kissed him wildly. "You were wonderful! I'm totally impressed."

He handed her the trophy. "This one's yours."

"I can't keep your trophy!"

"Sure you can." He unwrapped her scarf from his arm, looped it around the back of her neck, and pulled her against him. "You brought me luck."

"You didn't need me or my token tonight," she insisted.

He looked into her eyes, and for a moment the noise of the crowd faded. "You're wrong, April," he said. Her heart hammered crazily. "I need you more than you'll ever know."

10

After her first month of radiation, April returned to the city to meet with Dr. Sorenson. Her mother went with her and, after the routine exam, took her out for lunch and shopping. "I wish he'd told us something," her mother said as they settled into velvet-covered chairs at the restaurant.

"He did," April replied, nibbling on a bread stick. "He said there wasn't anything to tell us yet." Until her radiation therapy was completed, the tumor couldn't be measured, nor could she be given a prognosis report. To April's way of thinking, the visit had been a colossal waste of time. And with only three weeks until graduation, she'd have rather been spending the time at school.

Her mother studied the menu. "Nothing looks good to me. How about you?"

"I don't have much of an appetite. I think the treatments are affecting my taste buds. Everything tastes funny. Sort of dull."

"You should have said something to the doctor."

"It's normal, Mother," April said, although she didn't really think anything about cancer radiation was *normal*.

"You'll get through this, honey," her mother said sympathetically. She lowered her menu. "Oh, by the way, the Stevenses are having a dinner party Saturday evening and they've invited all of us."

The Stevenses were her parents' oldest and best friends, and April usually enjoyed attending their parties. "I can't. Mark's racing this Saturday and I'm going to cheer for him."

"You're certainly spending a lot of time with him."

April felt her radar go up. "And so what if I am?"

"You aren't dating the boys you used to date anymore."

"The boys I used to date are pretty juvenile, Mom."

"They were fine before."

"You mean before I got a brain tumor. They really can't relate to me anymore. High-school guys were fine until I got sick. Now they seem immature."

"But they're teenagers, April. Mark is a young man. What does he see in a girl your age?"

"Oh, thanks, Mother," April said sarcastically. "Maybe he actually *likes* me."

"You know what I mean." Her mother looked flustered, and bright spots of color appeared in her cheeks. "It merely seems odd that he's interested in dating someone four years younger than he is."

"Four years is nothing."

"Maybe you should give the boys from school another chance. Maybe you simply haven't found the right one."

Irritated, April declared, "Maybe I *have* found the right one. I care about Mark. And I'm not going to stop seeing him." Mark had come to mean a lot to her.

"Don't put words in my mouth. I didn't ask you to stop seeing him. I only questioned his motives."

"His motives?"

"Well, I wasn't born yesterday," her mother said in exasperation. "I know that young men don't always have pure and noble intentions."

"Are you saying you don't trust him? Or worse, that you don't trust me?"

"Of course I trust you. I've always trusted you. But you're . . . well . . . vulnerable now. You just said so."

April slumped back into her chair. "I can't believe we're having this conversation. I can't believe you're prying into my life."

"I'm not prying. I'm only making an observation."

"It hurts my feelings that you think Mark's an opportunist. He isn't after anything. He cares about me, and I don't think you should look for ulterior motives. It isn't fair."

April's mother sighed. "I don't want to fight with you, honey. I know what you're going through isn't easy. It isn't easy for your father and me either. You're our only child. A child we'd once given up hope of ever having. I think what's happened to you is one of life's cruelest tricks."

"You feel tricked? How?"

"I'm no stranger to problems, April. I'm

not naive enough to think that anybody goes through life without bumps and lumps. But after all we went through to conceive you, I thought the worst was over." Her mother shook her head. "Your father and I wanted you so badly and when we got you, we believed that you were a gift from heaven."

"Do you wish you never had me?"

"How can you even ask such a thing? You mean everything to us and we're so proud of you. I hate seeing you suffer. I'd give anything if it were me instead of you."

"But it *is* happening to me. I hate radiation. I hate knowing that something horrible is growing inside my head. It scares me."

"I'm scared too," her mother said quietly.

"And that's where Mark comes in," April added. "He makes me happy. He makes me feel less afraid. He makes me feel—" she started to say "loved" but stopped herself. *Love* was such a strong word. She wasn't sure that was how she felt about him yet. "He just makes me feel good about myself," she finished lamely.

"Then I won't hassle you about him. Because I want to see you happy."

Looking into her mother's eyes, April reconnected with the strong bond that had always existed between them. It had always been just the three of them, tightly knit with one another—Hugh and Janice and April— sometimes not knowing where one left off and the other began. Certainly she'd felt smothered by them occasionally. And she'd gone through phases of feeling awkward and embarrassed around them with her friends. But she had never defied them, or resented them, or wished she'd had other parents.

But something was happening between her and Mark. Something she couldn't explain but could only feel. Like a ship drifting away from a dock, her parents were diminishing in importance in her life. Her parents couldn't go with her. It was a journey she had to make without them.

"Don't these things look dorky?"

Kelli stood with April in April's bedroom, staring into a full-length mirror. They were both dressed in their caps and gowns. Graduation was only a week away.

"Pretty dorky," April agreed.

"So where are Armani and Chanel when you need them? Why haven't they tackled this fashion-design problem? I mean, anybody can create a dress or a suit, but a fashionable cap and gown—now, *that's* a challenge."

April chuckled. "These do make us look like cows, don't they?" She lifted the hem of her gown.

"And these hats! Why don't we just wear waffles on our heads? Then at least we could eat them after the ceremony."

April unzipped the navy blue gown and tossed it aside. "You know we have to go through with it. My father's already got the camcorder battery charged and reservations for dinner in the city."

"You aren't coming to Blair's party?" Kelli sounded disappointed.

"No."

"But why? It's going to be a blast."

"I don't mean to be a drag, Kelli, but I'm still not up to speed yet." April had completed radiation and it had left her feeling drained and tired. Now she wanted to rest and reorganize her life. And be with Mark. But she hesitated to say that to Kelli. "I feel as if I've missed out on the last six weeks of my life.

And trying to fit back in at a party isn't going to help."

"But everybody's missed you. I thought that once you were finished with your radiation you'd be right back into the swing of things."

"It's not that easy, Kelli." She did feel bad about isolating herself from her old friends, but it had been necessary. Unlike Mark, who'd desperately wanted to belong when he was growing up, April *had* belonged, but now wanted to be apart. She couldn't explain it. She hardly understood it herself. "High school's over. Nothing's going to be the same again anyway, so why should I try and recapture the past?"

"What about the plans we made for this summer? Do you want to chuck them too?"

"What plans?"

Kelli looked hurt. "The beach plans. When you missed the ski trip, you said you'd like to take a beach trip with the gang."

April thought about the beach, the warm sand and lapping waves. She *did* want to go. "I want to hit the beach."

Kelli's face broke into a grin. "I'll plan everything. I'll get the group together and we'll pick a week and find a place down the coast. I hear the beaches in North Carolina are fabulous. Why don't I check it out?"

"Go right ahead," April said with a smile. Her parents wouldn't object to her going. They knew her school friends and how much she enjoyed the ocean. And she figured that Mark wouldn't mind either. After all, it was only for a week.

But with a start she realized that there was one more person who had to okay her plans. Her doctor would have to give his permission too. Radiation might be over, but she still wasn't free to take charge of her future. It troubled her. The tiny blob at the base of her skull controlled her choices. And that was the most disturbing thing of all.

11

"Happy graduation, honey. Here's a little something from your mom and me." April's father opened a manila envelope and spread a handful of colorful travel brochures across the restaurant tablecloth.

"You're giving me brochures?" she teased. "How original, Daddy." The graduation ceremony was over. April had been one of three students in her class who received top academic honors. She had sent her college applications late, so she didn't know yet where she'd gotten in. But her academic honors, along with her high SAT scores, would improve her chances for entry into several elite schools.

"Not brochures," her father declared, "but a gateway to the world."

She studied the assortment. Greece, Hawaii, Italy, Japan, and China made an exotic fan on the tablecloth. He was offering her a trip to anywhere in the world she wanted to go. "I don't know what to say."

"Just pick your spot. I mean it, sweetheart. I'll take a month off and away we'll go," her father urged.

"How about a cruise to the Greek isles?" April's mother joined in.

"Or the Galápagos Islands," her father suggested. "Wouldn't you like to see the place that inspired Darwin to formulate his theory of evolution?"

"Hold it. We can't all just take off for a month. What about your job, Dad? And Mom, what about the store? What would Caroline say?"

"She's perfectly capable of running the store without me. And any place we go can be a potential treasure trove for the antique store. Why, a month hardly seems long enough. Why not longer?"

April shook her head. "Stop. Please. I appreciate the offer, but I don't want to go away right now. If I go anywhere, it'll be to the beach with my friends."

"But, honey, this is such a wonderful opportunity," said her mother. "You can do both."

"No, I can't."

"But we've always had such a good time on trips," her father interjected. "I thought it would be our last big vacation before you pack off to college."

But it wasn't college that April was thinking about. It was leaving Mark for a month. When they'd spoken on the phone the night before, he had sounded hoarse and wheezy. "Just a cold," he'd said, but she knew that for him a cold could turn into pneumonia. How could she leave him when the slightest complication could land him in the hospital? How could she expect to have a good time when she didn't know if he'd be well from day to day? The beach trip was local. She could return quickly if he had problems. If she was halfway around the world, it wouldn't be so easy.

"Can't we save the trip?"

"But why? You've always liked traveling with us before." Her mother sounded hurt.

"And I still do. Just not right now. It's my

final summer before college. I'd like to hang around, get reacquainted with my friends. The last few months haven't exactly been the most normal time of my life, you know."

Her parents exchanged glances; then her father said, "We don't want to pressure you into anything, April. We only thought an extended vacation would be a good way for you to put those months behind you."

"And," her mother added, "a way for us all to spend time together without the distractions of everyday life."

April couldn't help wondering how much her affection for Mark was entering into their decision. "I don't want to go." She shook her head stubbornly. "Not now. Maybe some other time."

"But—" her mother started.

Hugh Lancaster put a restraining hand on his wife's arm. "We can talk about it later. Tonight is supposed to be a celebration. Let's just have fun." He raised a glass of champagne in a toast. "To you, April. We're very proud of you."

"Yes, darling," her mother said. "*Very* proud."

April smiled at them, happy that the question of traveling with them could be set aside for the time being. Tomorrow night she'd be with Mark. *Mark*. The person who became more important to her with each passing day. The one person she wanted to be with more than any other.

Mark took her to the tiny Italian restaurant in his neighborhood that April had come to think of as their place. It wasn't fancy, but the food was delicious and the booths were encircled by red curtains, so they could be together in privacy. "Are you sure you feel up to eating out?" April asked.

"I'm doing better," Mark told her. "I'm on antibiotics and my respiratory therapist has been keeping a close watch on me. I'm going to be fine." He grinned, but she wasn't convinced.

"I'm not sure I believe you."

"Do you want me to prove it?"

"Right here in the restaurant?"

"The curtains are closed. We're alone."

"How can you?"

He reached into his coat pocket and pulled

out a red balloon. "Want to watch me blow this up?"

She stared. "Are you kidding?"

"Do I look like I'm kidding?" He took the balloon and gave a few puffs. It swelled, but April could see the effort it was costing him. She wanted to tell him to stop. It was painful watching him huff and puff to fill the balloon with his precious breath. But she knew she couldn't stop him. He was proving something to both of them, and she knew she must wait and watch and keep her mouth shut. At last, he tied the balloon and handed it over. "Told you I could do it."

Gold lettering on the balloon spelled out HAPPY GRADUATION, APRIL. A lump rose in her throat. "You couldn't have just bought me a card?"

He smiled, his face still flushed. "I made it in my uncle's print shop. Are you impressed?"

"Totally." She tied the balloon to the strap of her purse.

He reached for her hand. "After dinner, I have something else for you. It's a surprise."

April begged him to tell her what he was planning, but he wouldn't. She ate quickly, and when the meal was over they walked to his apartment, several blocks away. The summer city night felt steamy, and lights shone brightly from store windows. April had never been to Mark's apartment, and she was curious to see where he lived.

"My roommate's out," Mark said, unlocking the door. "I told him to make a night of it."

April's heart began to beat faster as he led her inside. The place was small and stuffy; an aging air conditioner struggled against the New York summer night. "Where's your room?"

He gestured toward a closed door.

"Can I see it?"

"It's a mess."

"But you're still going to let me see it."

"Maybe later. We've got a date up on the roof right now."

"We can go up there in a minute. I want to see your room first." He didn't budge. Slowly she said, "Come on, Mark. What's the big deal about me seeing your room?"

"My room . . . I told you, it's a mess."

"So what? My room's a mess too."

"Because it may scare you off."

"Is there a dead body in it?"

He laughed without humor. "Hardly."

"Then show me."

He led her to the door and opened it, and she stepped into his private world. At first glance, the room was ordinary. There were a bed, a dresser, a desk, and posters of beautiful racing cars on the walls. But she also saw that the top of his dresser was lined with medicine bottles. And there was a portable oxygen tank tucked into a corner near his bed. The odor of medicine hung in the air. "Welcome to my world," he said. "Just like everybody else's. Except for the CF."

She walked around it slowly. The number of medicine bottles stunned her, but she tried not to show it. She stopped in front of his desk, where a computer sat beside a pile of books, most of them about medicine. "I didn't know you were planning on going to medical school," she said.

"I'm not. But I study everything I can about my condition. I surf the Net looking for information too. I have friends in cyberspace. You know what's really nice about cyber-space?" April shook her head. "No one can see you. So everybody's equal. People only know you by your signon name."

"What's yours?"

"Speedman."

She chuckled. "Sounds like a superhero."

He stepped closer to her. "I'm no superhero. If I were, I'd be free of CF. You might say it's my personal form of kryptonite." He took her hand. "All this medicine just keeps me going."

"I'm glad you showed it to me."

"I had to."

"But why? You could have hidden the bottles."

"My mother cornered me last time I went to dinner. She said that if I cared about you—really cared—I should give you the total picture. Not just the fun stuff."

"We met in the hospital, remember? I already know you've got medical problems."

"More than problems, April. A lifelong condition. Barring some medical miracle, I'll never be well."

"Have you forgotten that I have a medical problem of my own?"

"I don't think of you as sick. It's possible for you to get well. Not me."

April swallowed hard. She knew it was true. "Why did you pick tonight to tell me all this? You must have a reason."

Mark's gaze never left her face. "Because I'm in love with you, April. And before we go any further, I need to know how you feel about me."

12

April's heart pounded and her mouth went dry. Mark loved her. Other boys had whispered those words to her, but always in the heat of passion, when they wanted to go further physically than she'd allow them. But Mark had said "I love you" in the cool light of reason. "I—I don't know what to say."

"Tell me how you feel."

"I feel like I need to sit down."

He searched her face. "Come to the roof with me. I've got something special up there for you."

They rode an elevator to the top floor, then trudged up a stairwell, their footfalls echoing behind them. April's head spun with the bombshell Mark had delivered. He loved her.

How did she feel? She knew she cared about him. But love? She wasn't sure.

He led her out onto the flat blacktopped roof above the city. Up there the air was cooler and the sound of the streets muffled. In the center of the roof, resting on a remnant of carpet, stood a table and two chairs. The table was draped with a cloth, and on top sat two candles, which Mark quickly lit. A small package wrapped in foil caught the candlelight and sparkled. Mark pulled out a chair for her.

A vase filled with roses scented the night air and stars twinkled overhead in a black velvet sky, like tiny jewels. A bouquet of balloons, all imprinted with the same message as the one Mark had given her earlier, was tied to her chair.

"You did all this for me?"

He just smiled.

She pointed to the balloons. "You didn't blow up all those, did you?"

"My uncle has a helium tank." Mark's grin was quick. "But thanks for thinking I could."

"Everything's perfect, Mark. Thank you."

"How can you say that? You haven't even opened your gift yet."

She fingered the small box. "You went to so much trouble."

"You're worth it."

With trembling fingers, she tore off the paper and lifted the lid of the box. Inside, on soft white cotton, lay a gold chain and a heart-shaped pendant—or rather half of a heart. The edges were jagged, as if the goldsmith had snapped it in two. Her name was engraved on the broken piece, the *i* in *April* dotted with a diamond chip.

Pulling his chair next to hers, Mark fished his key chain from his pocket. "Here's the other half," he said. On the chain, along with keys to his car, apartment, and garage, she saw the second half of the pendant, engraved with his name. Slowly he slid the two pieces together so that they fit neatly to form a complete golden heart. "Now it's perfect," he said. "Two halves equal one heart. That's how I feel about us. I was just half a person until you came along."

Too moved to speak, afraid her voice would break, April stared at the glittering jewelry. She had no words to tell Mark how much his gesture meant. He'd made her feel more special than any person had ever made her feel. Mark took the chain, drew it around her neck, and clasped it firmly in place.

He turned April to face him. "It looks just right on you."

She put her arms around his neck and buried her face in the hollow of his throat. The beat of her heart accelerated, and she knew that her next words would forever shape the course of their relationship. She knew that if she said them, she must *mean* them with all her heart. She pulled back and peered up at him. Candlelight played across the planes of his face, twinkling in his beautiful brown eyes. "Downstairs, you asked me how I felt about you. I can tell you now. Not because you've given me the sweetest, nicest gift I've ever received, but because I've been thinking about it for a long time."

She took a deep breath. "I love you, Mark. I never expected to, I never even wanted to. But I do."

His arms tightened around her, and she felt his warm breath on her neck. "I don't want you to think that telling me this makes me expect anything more from you."

"What do you mean?"

He held her at arm's length. "Just knowing you love me is its own reward. It's more than I ever hoped for."

She was confused. What was he trying to tell her? "Are you saying that hearing me say 'I love you' is all you want from me?"

"If I had my way, tonight would be the beginning for us. But I know you have plans, April. I know that you want to go to college and do other things with your life. It isn't fair for me to expect more."

That was true. She *did* want to go to college. She *did* want to pursue a career. And she still had a tumor growing inside her head. "How can telling you 'I love you' change my plans? Can't I still go to college and love you? Can't I still have a career and love you?"

"Once you get out in the world, your feelings for me may change."

"That can go both ways. What about your feelings for me?"

"My feelings for you are set in stone. They could never change. I'm just trying to let you know that I love you without strings attached."

"What kind of strings?"

He studied her for a long moment, and she

realized that he was struggling with what he wanted to say. From the street, she heard the wail of an ambulance pierce the night, and suddenly she knew what he wanted to tell her. "You don't want me to feel any obligation to you if you get really sick," she said slowly. "You want me to feel free to walk away."

He nodded. "That's exactly right. I have no right to ask anything from you. Not when I'm facing my particular future."

She never took her gaze from his face. "Don't you know, Mark? Love is a free gift. I can give it to you *if* I want to, *when* I want to, under *any* circumstances I want to." He stared at her, as if she might evaporate and float away. "Don't you believe me?" she asked.

He answered her by sweeping her into his arms and kissing her with an intensity that left her breathless.

"Your necklace is beautiful. Mark must be crazy about you," Kelli remarked.

April fingered the pendant around her neck. They were sunning themselves by the pool in April's yard. She'd already told Kelli about the romantic way Mark had given her his gift, without going into detail about his pledge of love for her. And now, days later, she still felt astounded. "He certainly surprised me with it."

"I'm glad it's him instead of Chris. I never thought Chris was the right one for you."

April rose on her elbows. "You never told me that before."

"You broke up with him, so I was never forced to tell you." Kelli dipped her hand into the water and swirled her fingers lazily. "I got an acceptance letter from the University of Oregon yesterday. It's my dad's alma mater, so it looks like that's where I'll be going."

"That's a long way off."

Kelli sighed. "I know. I won't get home except for Christmas and summer, but going so far away might be the best thing for me. At least I won't have to listen to my parents arguing all the time." Kelli had been unhappy at home for years. "It seems funny to be making plans that don't include each other."

"Yeah, I know. I mean, we've been in school together since the sixth grade. And now . . ." April let her sentence trail.

"How about you? You pick a college yet?"

April had received acceptance letters from

three colleges that week. "I've pretty much decided on Northwestern—it's outside of Chicago. They have top-notch journalism and broadcast schools."

"Chicago's where I'll have to change planes when I'm going to or coming from Oregon. Maybe you can meet me at the airport some-time."

"Maybe." April concentrated on the lap-ping sound of the water, suddenly saddened over the idea of her and Kelli's being so far apart. She slathered on more sunscreen, and the coconut scent reminded her of the beach. "By the way, how are things shaping up for our beach trip?"

"Not too good." Kelli sighed. "Cindy and Beth Ann took off for the summer. And Ashleigh is leaving this Friday to stay with her father and stepmother in Dallas."

"You're kidding! Except for you and me, there's no one left to go."

"They couldn't change their plans."

The news disappointed April, but what had she expected? "I guess when I became a her-mit they wrote me off. I guess I can't blame them."

"We can still go," Kelli offered. "But if we

do, it has to be soon. Dad's decided he wants to drive me and my stuff cross-country and visit some of his old friends on the way." Kelli rolled her eyes. "The university wants freshmen there early for orientation. We're leaving New York August first."

"But that's only six weeks away!" April cried in dismay.

"I know, but what can I do? Hey, how about this weekend? We could drive up the coast and find a comfy hotel on the water for a couple of days."

I have to go for outpatient testing with Dr. Sorenson on Friday, April thought, then asked, "How about during the week? The beaches would be less crowded then anyway."

"Sorry, I can't. Mom's dragging me shopping for clothes and dorm stuff."

April had to do the same things herself. She was excited about going, but also apprehensive. Chicago seemed very far from everything she knew and loved. And if the truth were known, she really didn't want to leave Mark. "So I guess the beach is out."

"How about July fourth weekend?"

"I can't. Mark is driving in a special race."

"Oh," Kelli said, sounding disappointed.

So the long-anticipated beach trip with her friends was out. April told herself not to act disappointed. She stretched out, resumed listening to the gently slapping water, and thought about the few weeks she had left with Mark. It wasn't going to be easy to leave him, but she was certain of her feelings for him. She loved him. And he loved her. Nothing else really mattered.

13

"**D**ad, you didn't have to come today. Mom and I can handle a visit to the doctor by ourselves." April and her parents were in Dr. Sorenson's waiting room at the hospital.

"No way," her father said, balancing his laptop computer on his knees. "I only have to answer some e-mail and do a spreadsheet for one client, so there's not much work to do. Besides I want to take my two favorite women out to dinner when this is over."

April's mother reached over and squeezed his hand, and April realized that he'd really come to lend moral support to his wife, which only made April feel more apprehensive. Did they suspect that the doctor was going to give them bad news? "It's going to be a long, boring day," April said.

"Hey, it's better than being cooped up in the office all day," he said brightly.

Mark had wanted to come also, but she'd told him not to. Her parents still weren't enthusiastic about her relationship with Mark. And to be honest, she had enough on her mind at the moment without dealing with any tension between Mark and her parents.

A nurse ushered them into an examination room. Dr. Sorenson said hello and began to write orders for her day of testing—blood work, X rays, CAT scan. "Will you be able to tell us anything today?" April asked.

He shook his head. "I'll have to evaluate the results and confer with my colleagues. Then we'll set up an appointment and go over everything with you."

"But how do you *think* I'm doing?" she pressed. "You must have some idea."

"I think you look terrific," he said with one of his professional smiles. "And you aren't having any more headaches, are you?"

"No, but—"

"Then let's wait until the results come in."

After a long day of tedious testing, her father took them to a Thai restaurant. April ate without tasting her food and pretended to be having a better time than she was. She didn't want to disappoint her parents, who kept saying, "No news is good news," and "I'm sure this is all behind us." She was glad when the evening was over and she was home again. She phoned Mark immediately.

"How long do you have to wait for the results?" he asked.

"Who knows? Maybe a week."

"Then stop thinking about it. Think about my big race. Think about you and me in the winner's circle. Think about all those new clothes you're going to buy for college. Think about how much fun we're going to have when I come visit you at Northwestern."

"All right, all right, enough," she said with a laugh. "I get the point: Think happy thoughts."

"It works for me. No matter how lousy I feel, I think of you and my whole day improves."

"You say the nicest things."

"Just the truth, and nothing but the truth."

On Monday April and her mother went into

the city and toured the big department stores, buying clothes for college. They also shopped for dorm-room accessories—comforter, sheets, towels, study lamp—everything the "Welcome Freshman" letter she'd received from the registrar suggested. With every purchase, she felt a mounting excitement. In two months she'd be settling into a brand-new life, and except for missing Mark, she was looking forward to it.

She had her mother drop her off at Mark's afterward. "He'll bring me home," she said.

Her mother peered up at the aging apartment building. "Are you sure this place is safe?"

"Of course it's safe. Everybody can't live in Woodmere," April said, naming their exclusive Long Island suburb.

Her mother insisted on coming up with her. They took the elevator to Mark's floor and rang the bell. When the door opened, Mark stood there in his bare feet. He looked flushed and his breath sounded raspy. "You're early," he said, clearing his throat.

Feeling her mother eyeing him, April asked, "Is it okay? We can come back later."

"Come in. Randy was just finishing up my therapy."

Randy sauntered out of Mark's bedroom and gave April a cheerful smile. "I'm out of here." He turned to Mark. "See you later, man."

"What therapy?" April's mother asked once the three of them were alone.

"Respiratory," Mark said. "To break up . . . well . . . to help me breathe better. My lungs get clogged. Want some iced tea?"

"No, thank you." She gazed around the apartment, and April could tell she wasn't overly impressed. "How long have you been living here?"

"Two years. It's not permanent. I have plans to move to a better place."

April's mother walked to the makeshift bookshelves across the room. She stood examining Mark's racing trophies. "It looks as if you've won a lot of races."

"Well . . . a few."

April stepped in front of her mother before she could go back to giving Mark the third degree. "Aren't you supposed to meet Dad for supper?"

"What about your supper?"

"I'm cooking," Mark said with a disarming grin. "I'm not a bad cook. My Mom's Italian and I learned from her."

April could see that her mother was hesitant. April promised to be home before midnight and nearly pushed her mother out the door.

"I don't think she was happy about leaving you here," Mark said when he and April were alone.

"She knows I come here a lot. Today shouldn't make any difference."

"But this is the first time she's seen my place. I don't think she likes it. I can't blame her. You deserve better."

"Get real! Mom's just being Mom. Frowning and disapproving is her natural state." April tried to joke about it.

Mark didn't seem to believe her. "I wish things were different. I wish I had more to offer you."

"What do you mean? What would you offer me?"

He shrugged. "Forget it. You'll be out of here soon and I'll be just a memory."

"Please don't say that."

"Look, I'm sorry. I don't mean to be such a downer. Let's get into the kitchen and see what I can put together. I promised your mother I'd feed you, and I will. I really am a good cook."

She caught his arm. "I'd rather do something else instead."

"What?"

She took a deep breath. "I've been thinking about it for a while, and now seems like the best time to bring it up. You've shut me out of your CF world, Mark."

"What do you mean?"

"I want to learn how to do your thumps. Just like Randy does."

Mark shook his head. "No."

"Why not? I want to learn. I want to help. I hate having to end our evenings early because Randy has to pound your back. Or get a late start because he has to work on you first. I can learn, Mark. I can do it for you and—"

"No!" His tone was firm and sharp. "That's not what I want from you, April. I don't want you to be my nurse."

"You tell me you love me, but you won't let me share this with you. That's not fair." She heard her voice rising. "If we love each other,

then you should let me into this part of you.
It's a big part, Mark."

He looked away from her. "The answer is
no. I don't want you to see me that way."

"But I saw you in the hospital."

"Not the same thing."

"But—"

He took her by her shoulders, pulled her
against his chest, wrapped his arms around
her, and held her so tightly she could scarcely
breathe. "Please, April. Please understand. I
love you too much to fight with you. Just
don't ask this of me. My therapy is not something I want you to do for me. I want you to
love me, not nurse me."

She didn't want to be shut out of any part
of his life but decided against arguing with
him about it just now. He wanted to spare
her, shield her from his fragility. But his stub-
bornness was driving a wedge between them,
and she couldn't make him see it. "I love you,
Mark," she whispered. "And nothing's going
to change that. Nothing."

Three days later, Dr. Sorenson called April
and her parents into his office for a confer-
ence. He shuffled papers, steepled his fingers,

and studied them across the expanse of his cluttered desk. April knew right away the news wasn't good.

"We aren't seeing the kind of progress that we'd hoped to see in reducing the tumor," he said. A fluorescent bulb buzzed noisily overhead, reminding April of a fly trapped on window glass.

"What does that mean?" Her father asked cautiously. Her mother sat tense and white-lipped.

"It hasn't shrunk appreciably."

"You mean I went through all those weeks of radiation and it didn't help?" April felt numb and detached, as if she were discussing some other person.

"That is correct."

"So I still can't have the gamma knife surgery?"

"Very few neurosurgeons would attempt such a surgery. It's not just the size of the tumor. It's the placement—its growth around the brain stem and cerebellum."

"But I want it out! I want it gone!"

Her mother gripped her hand until April's fingers ached. "What if you did the surgery anyway?" her mother asked.

"We could paralyze her. Or even kill her."

Her father cleared his throat. "All right, you've made your point. So, tell us, where do we go from here? More radiation?"

"Radiation didn't work, and because she also had radiation as a child, we can't put her through that protocol again."

"Then what?" April had to clench her teeth to talk, afraid they would chatter because she was shaking all over.

"The tumor is dormant right now, and it could remain so."

"For how long?"

Dr. Sorenson shook his head. "I don't know. I wish I had better news for you."

He was being purposely evasive and it frightened April. "I'm supposed to go away to college. I've been accepted to Northwestern."

"You don't have to change your plans. Chicago has fine neurologists, and I can get you the name of someone to take over your case."

"No." April stood. "*You* just want to be rid of me because *you* can't fix me."

Dr. Sorenson's face reddened. "That's not true, April."

She turned to her parents, who looked ashen. "I don't have anything left to say to this man. Except, thanks for nothing!" She spun on her heel and stalked from the room.

14

April ran out of the hospital, hailed a cab, and gave the driver Mark's address. She knew his schedule by heart now and was sure he'd be at home. She needed to see him. *Had* to see him. Tears blurred her eyes, and she felt as if a hundred-pound weight were pressing on her chest.

At his apartment, she rang the doorbell. She fidgeted on his doorstep until he opened the door. "April!"

"Mark . . ." April's voice quivered as she tried to tell him what had happened at the doctor's office.

"Come in, honey. Tell me what's going on." Inside, he settled beside her on the couch. "Your doctor didn't give you good news, did he?"

Too choked with emotion to speak, April shook her head. Mark held her close while she cried and sputtered out her story bit by bit. "I'm no better, Mark. No better at all," she finished. "Nothing they did for me has helped."

"Maybe you didn't hang around long enough to hear everything your doctor had to say."

"The expression on his face said it all. He didn't give me any hope because there isn't any."

She watched Mark's eyes fill with tears. "I won't accept that. I won't lose you."

"Aren't we the perfect couple?" she whispered. "You think you have no future, but I don't seem to have one either."

He grabbed her shoulders. "Stop that kind of talk! You don't know your future. The radiation could have damaged the tumor and stopped its growth. It may never flare up again. You may live to be ninety."

April's thoughts were reeling. Deep down, she'd assumed that modern medicine would fix her as it had the first time. That the radiation would have shrunk the tumor enough for surgical removal. She hadn't been prepared to hear that it hadn't worked. "What am I going to do?"

"You don't have to make plans for the rest of your life right this minute. You just have to get through the next minute and then the one after that. That's how I do it."

April realized that every time Mark got sick, he stood at the very crossroads where she now stood. He wondered if he would ever have a tomorrow, ever make plans for a future. Yet he never seemed depressed. He'd shown her that life could be good in spite of bleak medical problems. Mark was strong in a way that April saw she too must be. She couldn't give up. She wouldn't. She took a deep breath. "I feel like I'm going to explode."

"That feeling I can help you with," he said, smoothing her hair. "When things look really bad for me, I drive fast."

"Aren't there laws about speeding?"

"Only if they catch you."

He drove her in his aqua and white Chevy onto the interstate and out into the countryside, turning off onto side roads and finally stopping on what looked like a deserted airstrip. Weeds grew out of the cracked concrete. Mark shut off the engine and turned to her. "This is where I learned to drive. The surface is still decent."

"What do you want me to do?"

"Take the wheel."

"Me? You want me to drive your car?"

"Drive her fast."

"But I can't—"

"Sure you can."

He got out of the car. "Come on, switch places with me." April slid over into the driver's seat, and Mark got into the passenger's seat. She switched on the engine. It rumbled, low and velvety. She let the clutch out slowly and the car eased forward. It felt like a racehorse coiled and waiting to sprint. She pressed on the gas pedal, felt the car lurch, and glanced at Mark. He grinned.

She pulled out onto what had once been a runway. She shifted gears and felt the car gather speed. She shifted again and pushed the pedal lower. Forty, sixty, seventy—the speedometer's needle climbed. She gripped the wheel with both hands, braking as she came to the end of one runway and turning onto another.

Eighty, ninety . . . the speedometer inched higher. The field on either side of the strip became a streaking blur. Her fear faded. She thought of nothing except pushing the car faster. It was pure exhilaration. The engine roared. The needle hit 100, but then a curve forced her to brake and send the needle downward into the 70s.

As she pushed the car along the crisscrossing surfaces of long, deserted runways, her mind emptied of her troubles. Nothing else mattered but the speeding car. Every nerve ending was focused on keeping the car going fast. The tires hit breaks in the concrete, making the car vibrate and making her hold on tighter. And push harder. Finally, exhausted, she slowed, downshifted, and braked.

Her knuckles were white. She'd been gripping the wheel so hard that she'd lost all sensation in her hands. Perspiration poured off her face and neck. Breathing hard, she leaned back against the leather upholstery. The roar in her ears went quiet, so quiet she thought she'd gone deaf. During the drive, she'd forgotten everything. The brain tumor. The doctor's bleak report. Her plans for college. Her family, her friends, even Mark. It all had melted into the white blur of speed and heat and the sound of a racing engine and the smell of gasoline. She turned toward Mark.

His face was awash in afternoon sunlight. He was smiling, and his dark brown eyes danced. "Now you know why I do it."

Later, as he drove her home, April's fear returned. Where had she gotten the nerve to drive so fast? What if she'd crashed? Wrecked his car? She might have killed both herself and Mark! Yet she had tempted fate. And she'd won. She was still alive. She smiled and caught sight of her reflection in the glass window. She looked disheveled but glowing. Mark had given this to her. He had understood exactly what she'd needed to once again feel in control of her life.

It was almost dark when she made him drop her off at the top of her driveway. "Go on home," she said. "I have to face my parents by myself."

"I'll go with you."

She stroked his arm. "This is my battle. I'll call you later."

When she walked through the door, her parents threw themselves at her. "Where have you been? We've been worried sick about you!"

"I went to see Mark."

"Mark! You left us sitting there in the doctor's office. We didn't know where you'd gone, what had happened to you."

"Don't ever do that to us again, April," her father growled.

"I'm sorry I worried you," April said, feeling guilty. "I guess I just figured you'd realize where I'd gone."

"No," her mother said, shrilly. "We didn't realize."

"I said I was sorry." She glanced at them, seeing their anxiety but feeling annoyed. "I'm not a child, you know. I'm almost eighteen."

"You're *our* child." Her father's voice rose. "And I don't care how old you get, we'll always be concerned about you. We all heard some pretty jolting news today. Don't you think we were affected by it too?"

"Yes." She felt tears stinging her eyes, but she didn't want to break down and cry. The exhilaration of the drive was evaporating, and she couldn't hold on to it when her parents kept jerking her back into their reality. "I said I was sorry."

Her father's scowl lessened, and he took her into his arms. "We love you, April. And I don't want you to think for a minute that what the doctor said today is the final word. There are other doctors, other treatment centers. I've placed some calls to European facilities. They don't have to deal with the FDA, so sometimes their treatment techniques and medical protocols aren't as rigid as ours over here."

No! April thought. She didn't want to spend months trekking all over the globe looking for some elusive cure when all that she loved and cared about was right here. "Well, Dr. Sorenson did say that the tumor was dormant now. I think that's a good sign . . . don't you?"

"I do," her mother said. "I think we have to concentrate on the positive aspects."

Her father stepped away, raked his hands

through his graying hair, and said, "Of course we will. I just don't want April to feel as if she's been robbed of hope."

"I still have hope," she assured him. "I see how Mark makes it through a day at a time. And that inspires me. I'll make it through that way too."

"And about college—"

"Not now." April interrupted her mother. "I can't think about that now."

Her father left the room, and her mother sat with her on the sofa. They sat quietly, with only the ticking of the grandfather clock across the room breaking the silence. The tension of the day overcame April, and suddenly she felt exhausted. She put her head back and closed her eyes.

"You really like this boy, don't you?"

April tensed. "I thought we already talked about Mark and me."

"But your feelings for him have deepened, haven't they?"

April heard a melancholy note in her mother's words, and April wondered what she was expected to say. "I like him." She took a deep breath, knowing it was time to be completely truthful. "Actually, I love him."

"*Love*'s a serious word. I've never heard you use it with anybody except family."

"I've never felt this way about anybody else before."

"April, don't—"

"No, Mom, *you* don't." April struggled to her feet. "You don't know what I'm feeling. But I do, so please don't lecture me about my emotions. My whole life changed today. I don't know what it means yet, but I just know things aren't going to move along the way you, Dad, and I had planned them. I need time to think. I need space. And right now, Mark's the only person in the world who understands me."

Without waiting for her mother to reply, April darted from the room and ran up the stairs and into her bedroom, where she threw herself across her bed and wept bitterly.

15

It took April three weeks to decide that she wasn't going to go away to college. Dr. Sorenson's analysis of her case had dashed many of her dreams and ambitions. She knew her parents were relieved because they hadn't wanted her to be far away, but they were also upset because college had been in their plans for her ever since she was born. "We'll find someplace local," her father said. "Good heavens, we live in New York, there are plenty of choices."

"Sure," April said, forcing herself to sound cheery. "Maybe I'll take a few courses—you know, the things every freshman has to take, and then transfer somewhere in January."

Ever since April's argument with her

mother, her parents had been walking on egg-shells around her. They had nothing more to say about Mark, which helped her feel less boxed in and defensive, but she knew they'd discussed it between themselves many times. Just as long as they left her alone, she didn't care what they talked about.

On the morning when Kelli was leaving with her father to drive out to Oregon, April showed up in her friend's driveway. They stood beside the trailer hooked to the back of Kelli's father's car, waiting for him to finish up details inside the house. April eyed the trailer solemnly. "I'll bet it's full."

"To the brim. I didn't realize how much of my stuff I wanted to take with me."

"You are planning on coming back, aren't you?"

Kelli cast a furtive glance toward her house. "If I have a place to come back to."

"Are things that bad?"

"I think Dad's using this trip as an excuse to check out his options." April didn't know what to say, but Kelli changed the subject. "I'm going to miss you."

"Same here."

"You are going to be all right, aren't you?"

"As all right as I can be under the circumstances." When she'd first told Kelli about her visit to Dr. Sorenson, her friend had burst into tears, and it had been April who'd ended up comforting Kelli instead of the other way around.

"At least you have Mark," Kelli said. "I'm glad you do."

"Me too. At least some part of my life is perfect."

The front door opened and Kelli's father came out, juggling a Thermos of coffee and a set of road maps. Kelli's mother was right behind him. April waited while Kelli hugged her mother goodbye. Then she hugged her friend. "You write me," Kelli said. Tears brimmed in her eyes.

"I will. You write too." April sniffed. Saying goodbye was harder than she'd imagined.

Kelli climbed into the car, and April called, "See you at Christmas." A lump rose in April's throat. She was supposed to be going away too, and for the first time it struck her how completely her life had changed. She stepped back and stood shoulder to shoulder with Kelli's mother, watching the car and trailer pull slowly out of the driveway and out of her life.

Over the next several weeks, April said goodbye to many of her friends and watched them head off to college, while she enrolled in only two classes at NYU. Freshman orientation was a bewildering maze that left her tired and short-tempered, but Mark picked her up afterward and took her to their favorite little restaurant, where he soothed her with a plate of linguine and a chocolate torte. "Feel better?" he asked as she finished the meal.

"Much. But if I continue to eat like this, you'll have to get a tow truck to drive me around."

He smiled. "I'd love you even if you grew another head."

"I'll keep it in mind." He'd been unusually quiet. "Want to tell me what's bothering you?"

"What makes you think something's bothering me?"

"Isn't something?"

He shrugged, looked sheepish, and said, "I guess I've been thinking about you starting classes. And about all the new guys you'll be meeting."

"Oh, sure. Right. I'm having to beat them off with a stick already."

"I'm serious, April. You're beautiful, and it won't be long before some guy notices and asks you out."

Half exasperated, she said, "So what's your point? Do you want me to say yes?"

"Of course not. But I don't want you to feel obligated to me either."

Completely exasperated now, she snapped, "Is that what you think of me? That I date you because I feel obligated? That's idiotic, Mark! And insulting. Especially after all we've been through together."

"Don't be mad."

"I don't know what else to be. You're really upsetting me."

He rested his elbows on the table and leaned toward her. "That is the last thing I ever wanted to do. I don't know why I'm acting like such a jerk. Forgive me. Okay?"

She couldn't stay angry with him, but she didn't want to let him off too easily either. "So, will you please get over your problem already? I don't know how else to show you I care about you. About us. I don't know what else I can say."

He studied her intently. "All right. Fair enough. I won't question your feelings again." He paused, stared at her thoughtfully, then asked, "Do you believe in love at first sight? I do. And the first time I looked up and saw you across that hospital waiting room, I was dazzled. I know that must sound stupid, but it's the truth. When my grandmother was alive, she used to tell me that every time God creates a soul in heaven, he creates another to be its special mate. And that once we're born, we begin our search for our soul mate, the one person who's the perfect fit for our mind and body. The lucky ones find each other."

Moved, she reached across the table and took his hand. "Mark, I know that we have a place in each other's lives. And no matter what happens, I will never forget you. And I will never feel quite the same way about anybody else again. You are my first—no—you are my *only* love."

His eyes filled with tears and, embarrassed, he glanced away. When he spoke, his voice was gruff. "Come on, let's get out of here. I want to hold you and kiss you and if I do it here—well, we may have to find another restaurant to call ours."

She stood with him, and arm in arm they walked to the cashier, paid, and walked out into the moonlight.

On September fourth Mark turned twenty-two, and his parents threw a family birthday party. Their small house was filled with aunts, uncles, and cousins. Mark's mother cooked platters of food along with several desserts, including an enormous cake that sat in the center of the dining room table. Balloons, trailing long ribbons, floated against the ceiling, and a birthday banner stretched from one side of the dining room to the other. "Having a good time?" Mark yelled to April above the noise of the celebration.

"Terrific!" she answered. When it came time to open presents, she sat on the floor by his feet handing him gifts from a large pile on a nearby table. She held her gift back, waiting until most of the others were opened. Finally she pushed the giant, beautifully wrapped box toward him.

"Open it," April urged, anxious for Mark to see her present.

He ripped off the wrapping paper, reached into the box, and pulled out a complete racing suit made of a flame-retardant fabric. The silvery white material of the coveralls, helmet, and gloves caught the light as he held them up. His jaw dropped. "This is awesome." He stared down at her. "These things cost a fortune!"

"You're worth it," she said, satisfied with his reaction and knowing she'd caught him totally off-guard.

Mark jumped up and held the outfit for all to see. "Look at this! It's the best stuff made for racing today."

She grinned, but stopped grinning when she saw the expression on Mark's mother's face. She was not smiling. She was not one bit impressed with April's gift. April realized that she had only been thinking of what Mark would like when she'd chosen the gift. She'd forgotten how his mother might react.

Later, when April was helping to stack dishes in the kitchen, Rosa said to her, "I know what you gave Mark cost a great deal of money."

"The money isn't important. I picked something that I knew he'd like. I know you don't approve of his racing, but the suit will make it safer. I mean, I worry about him too. I'm sorry if it upset you."

Rosa studied April. "I realize Mark's a grown man. And I know how much his racing means to him. I'm not trying to be an over-protective mother, but put yourself in my place. When he was diagnosed with CF as a little boy, his doctor told us that he probably wouldn't live beyond his sixteenth birthday."

April sucked in her breath. "Really?"

"I never dreamed he'd see twenty-two. Every year now is a special gift from God. What upsets me about the racing is that every time he goes out on that track, he's flirting with death."

"He's a good driver."

"I know he is. But why court disaster? It scares me to watch him drive. That's why I stopped going to the track to watch him. When he began dating you, I thought he might give up the racing."

"I don't think that's going to happen," April replied. "I think the racing sort of balances out the CF in his mind. He can't change his medical condition, but he can affect how fast he pushes his car. Pushing the car to its limit makes him feel in control.''

"You're right. But I can't . . ." Mark's mother's voice trailed off, and April could see that the conversation was making Mrs. Gianni very emotional.

"I understand," April told her. "But for him, it's worth the risk. And neither of us really has the right to rob him of that sense of power.''

Rosa slipped a pile of dishes into a sinkful of water. "Life never balances out, April. At best, it simply lets you coast along with the illusion of control. At worst, it wrenches control from you totally and then you have to decide how you're going to deal with it.''

"Well, I think Mark deals with it by not giving up. And by making plans and acting on them.''

"And you?" Rosa asked. "How do you deal with it?''

April knew that Mark's family was aware of her medical problems. She replied, "One day at a time. Mark taught me that.''

"You're a lovely girl, April, but you've lived a very privileged life. Mark hasn't.''

April was taken aback. "Privilege doesn't make a difference when you get sick, Mrs. Gianni. Or when you get diagnosed with a brain tumor. And all the money in the world can't make either thing go away. So Mark and I are more alike than we are different."

Rosa was about to reply, but the kitchen door swung open and a group of relatives entered, chattering and carrying plates and left-over food. April never knew what Mark's mother might have said, but she did get the impression that it wouldn't have been approving. And she wondered why, after all these months, his mother seemed against April being with her only son.

16

"What were you and my mother talking about in the kitchen?" Mark fumbled with the key to his apartment, his arms heaped with birthday gifts. "I stuck my head into the kitchen and saw that she had you cornered."

April unlocked the door for him. "Girl talk. Nothing important."

"That's hard to believe. She was trying to make you pressure me to give up racing, wasn't she?" He switched on a table lamp, and soft light filled the room.

"It's no secret that she'd rather you didn't race. What's that?" She pointed to an enormous box perched in the middle of the sofa.

"Why don't you check it out?"

She read the tag. "It's for me. And it's from

you." He grinned mischievously. "Why would I get a present? It's *your* birthday."

"Haven't you heard? It's better to give than to receive."

"What are you up to, Mark Gianni?"

"Guess you'll have to open it to find out."

She bounced onto the sofa and studied the box. "Your box for me is bigger than my box for you. Did you get me a racing suit too?" She tore off the outer wrapping, opened the flaps of the box, and discovered—another wrapped box. "What's this?"

He shrugged. "I guess you'll have to keep unwrapping."

Intrigued, she tore off the next box's layer of paper. Inside she found another box. "You're driving me crazy! Is that what you want? A crazy girl on your hands?"

He laughed. "Boy, you get cranky over the smallest details."

She tossed a wad of wrapping paper at him and ripped open the next box. Inside it was another. And inside that, another still. She unwrapped ten boxes in all, until one very small one lay in the palm of her hand. "I know," she sighed. "It's an Elvis postage stamp, isn't it?"

"Only one way to find out," he replied.

She ripped off the paper and discovered a small black velvet box. But there the game ended. Inside this box, nestled in folds of white satin, lay a gold antique-looking ring with a diamond in its center. She gasped and, wordlessly, turned toward him. Mark had sunk to one knee beside the sofa. He took her hand, and his brown eyes stared directly into hers. "Marry me, April. I love you, and more than anything in the world, I want you to be my wife."

She began to cry.

"I was hoping for a different reaction," he said, looking crestfallen.

A million emotions tumbled through her—love, excitement, awe, joy . . . fear. "Mark, I don't know what to say."

" 'Yes' would be nice. I love you, April. I thought you loved me too."

She cupped his face in her hands. "Of course I love you. And, yes, I will marry you."

His face broke into a grin, and his eyes sparkled. He slid the ring on her finger. The diamond caught the lamplight and twinkled brilliantly. "I know the stone's small, but it

once belonged to my grandmother. She left it
to me in her will because she always believed
that somewhere God had picked out one special girl for me. And she was right."

April blinked back tears. "It's perfect. And
I'm honored to wear it."

"I wish she could have known you. She
would have loved you too."

April couldn't take her eyes from the glittering stone on her hand. *Engaged!* She was
engaged to Mark Gianni.

"When can we get married?" he asked.

"I don't know. There's so much to think
about . . . so much to do," she said, still fas-
cinated with the diamond. But in the back of
her mind, she knew her parents might not be
enthusiastic about her acceptance of Mark's
proposal. They would say she was young. That
she had four years of college ahead of her. She
realized she had a brain tumor that might begin growing once more.

Mark smoothed her hair. "Now that I know
you'll marry me, I don't want to wait." He
kissed her, long and sweet. Her heart hammered, and she clung to him while visions of
herself in a long white wedding gown danced
through her head.

The dream ended abruptly the next morning when she told her parents about Mark's proposal. Her mother's face went pale, her father's livid. "You can't be serious!" he said.

April had known they would object. Still, she was determined to marry Mark. "I am serious. What's wrong with us getting married?"

"You're not even eighteen," her father railed. "You're still a child."

She rolled her eyes. "Please. Mom was nineteen when you married her."

"That was different."

Her mother jumped in. "April, how can you think about marrying a man like Mark, who may die at any time?" Her voice was quiet, but it cut through April like a knife.

"Anyone can die at any time," she answered coolly.

"His odds are higher than most and you know it."

"My odds aren't the greatest either," she said. "Or have you forgotten?"

"You're in remission," her father insisted. "And you may remain so forever. And what of your other plans? You just enrolled in college."

"I can be married and still go to college."

"How will he provide for you? He works in a print shop, for heaven's sake. And he plays with cars on the side. Do you know how expensive it is to live in New York? Have you any idea—?"

"Stop it!" She put her hands over her ears. "I won't listen to you tear down Mark another minute." She whirled and ran up the stairs. She threw herself on the bed and seethed. This was supposed to be a happy day. Instead, her parents had turned it into a fight. Why couldn't they be happy for her?

She ignored the soft knock on the door, but her mother came into the room anyway. "I should have locked it," she whispered through clenched teeth. "Go away."

Her mother sat on the bed. "I came to talk, not argue." Her voice was soft, and she sounded weary. "April, I know you think we're being unreasonable, but we honestly have your best interests at heart."

"How can you? I love Mark and you hate him."

"That's simply not true. We like Mark. We just think you're too young to make this kind of commitment. In spite of what you see in bride magazines, once the wedding day is over a couple has to live in reality."

"You're arguing. You told me you wouldn't."

Her mother sighed. "Then let me cut to the chase. Marriage is hard enough without any obstacles. You and Mark have considerable obstacles. Cystic fibrosis is a bad disease and its victims need plenty of care."

"I know what Mark needs." April cut her off. "He needs special medications. He needs therapy. I plan to learn how to do his back and chest thumps. I can handle it."

"It isn't some little thing, like brushing your teeth at night or washing your face every morning. It's serious, life-sustaining business. It means that no matter how tired you are, no matter if you've had a fight and the two of you are angry with each other, no matter what, you have to perform this procedure."

"I can handle it," April said stubbornly. But she knew her mother was right. The responsibility was weighty. "Besides, I'm sure his respiratory therapist won't drop out of Mark's life entirely. He'll still be in the picture."

"There are other things about boys with CF—"

"I don't want to hear about it!"

"Maybe you should talk to his mother. I have."

April jumped off the bed. "You *what?* You've gone to Mark's family behind our backs? I don't believe it! How could you?" Suddenly Rosa's attitude toward April after the birthday party made perfect sense. April's mother had gone to see her. Who knew what her mother may have said?

"Because I love you!" her mother replied. "Because I don't want to see you get in over your head."

"Stop treating me like a baby! I'm old enough to get married if I want to."

"Not without our permission, you're not." Her mother was standing too, and they'd squared off, facing each other.

"I'm going to marry Mark," April said in clipped words. "Whether you and Dad approve or not. I love him and he loves me. We'll get by. I'd rather have your blessing, but I'll do it without if I have to. And if we have to run away to do it, we will. That's a promise."

———

"Engaged!" Kelli squealed over the phone. April had called Kelli in Oregon as soon as her mother had left the bedroom. "That's so awesome!"

"Tell that to my parents," April said.

"They're not glad about it?"

"It's like a war zone around here, although there's a temporary truce right now because they hate upsetting me." April made a face. "I think they're giving me time to 'come to my senses.' But I'm not going to change my mind. Which is one reason I'm calling. If we work this out, will you be my maid of honor?"

Kelli squealed again. "You bet!"

Her enthusiasm warmed April's heart. "So, how's college life?"

"The classes are harder than high school. The campus is huge. And it rains every day."

"But you like it?"

"It's okay. Lots of cute guys around."

April felt a pang of longing. *For what?* she asked herself. Her life was different now; her plans a hundred and eighty degrees from what they'd been even six months before. By the same time a year from now, she'd hopefully be married. No, it wasn't what she—or her parents—had once planned for her. But the new direction pleased her.

"They'll come around," Kelli said across the miles, as if reading April's thoughts. "Your parents will do anything for you, so don't get too bent out of shape. I'm telling you, they'll do this for you too."

17

"I'm sorry this is causing problems between you and your parents. I never meant for that to happen," Mark said.

Late-afternoon sun sparkled on the lake in Central Park, where April and Mark had met after her class at NYU. They sat on a bench, watching geese swim through the sunlit water; the air felt crisp and smelled of autumn. The sky was a brilliant shade of icy blue, and the trees were already tinged with gold and red.

"Kelli thinks they'll come around," April said. She held Mark's hand. "I think she's right. I just wish they'd hurry up about it. I bought one of those bridal books, and there's so much to do before the ceremony. The book says you should start up to a year in advance to plan your wedding."

"A year? I don't want to wait a whole year."

"Neither do I. So I skipped those pages. We can do it in six months, but we need to start now."

"Is it that important to you? I mean, that we have a big wedding?"

"I don't know. I—I just wish Mom and I were planning it together. It would be so much easier. And a whole lot more fun." Weeks after April had announced her intention to marry Mark, her parents still hadn't warmed to the idea. It hurt her to have them act indifferent about it. Her mother had gone off on a fall buying tour for the antique store and her father was busy with a rash of new clients. April couldn't have discussed it with them even if she'd wanted to. A gust of cool wind chilled her, and she edged closer to Mark. "How about your family? How do they really feel about it?" His parents had seemed excited about the news, but she didn't know what they might be saying to Mark behind her back.

"Actually, they're okay about it. Ma's already been to talk to the priest, and as long as we get married in the church, there won't be any problems. But then, the groom's family doesn't have much to do anyway. It's the bride's show."

"There's the rehearsal dinner," she reminded him.

"No problem. Ma's already looking for a place to have it, but you'll have to tell her how many people to plan for."

"See, that's what I mean. There are so many details. I can't even come up with a guest list without my mother's help." Out on the lake the geese rose into the sky, honking and flapping gray and black wings. "Did you know my mother went to talk to yours a few weeks back?"

"Ma told me the other day."

"I can't believe her! She makes me so angry."

"She's just concerned about you."

"Why are you taking her side?"

"I'm not. It's just that I understand. I have CF, April. It's a big deal and she has a right to be concerned."

"I'm tired of everybody's concern," she said peevishly. "I can think and act for myself. I have to learn how to take care of you, you know. I have to learn how to do your thumps."

Mark sighed, rested his forearms on his knees, and stared at the ground. "I know. But it scares me."

"Are you afraid I'll be incompetent?"

"No. I'm afraid you'll be grossed out."

Her irritability vanished, and her heart went out to him. She slid her arm around his waist and rested her cheek against his hunched shoulder. "You could never gross me out. I love you."

He straightened and drew her into his arms. In spite of their heavy jackets, she felt the warmth of his body. "Come home with me tonight. After dinner, Ma will show you what you'll need to know."

"I could learn from Randy," she ventured.

"He'll instruct you too. But we'll start with my mother. She's done it all my life, so she'll be the best teacher."

April nodded. She couldn't admit she was scared, but she was. Could she learn to do his thumps correctly? What if she messed up? She pushed aside her fears. Mark needed her. She wasn't going to let him down. She was going to be his wife.

Overhead, the geese circled in V-formation, honking goodbye forlornly.

That night, April watched Mark's mother pound his chest and then his back with cupped hands and a steady rhythm. Mark coughed and gagged and spit up phlegm. April steeled herself, telling herself that this was a way of life for him and once they were married, it would become her responsibility.

"Now you try it," Rosa directed April.

April cupped her hands and slapped Mark's back.

"Harder," Mark said. "You have to hit harder."

Rosa explained, "You can only hurt him if you don't get the phlegm good and loose. It's got to be broken up and expectorated."

By the time the session was over, perspiration poured off April. Her palms stung and her shoulders ached from leaning over Mark. He straightened, breathing hard, his voice raspy. "That's enough." He went into the bathroom, and April heard him brushing his teeth.

"Are you going to be all right?" Rosa asked.

April reddened. "Sure. Don't worry. I'll get the hang of it."

"It was difficult for me at first too. He was two when he was diagnosed and I had to pound him so hard on the back I was afraid I'd hurt him. At first his father had to hold him down. But he soon got with the program. In a few months, he simply lay down on the pillows for me. He doesn't ever remember another way of life, except to get thumped several times a day." Rosa shook her head. "But when you love your child, you'll do anything for him."

"Was it hard for you when Mark moved out on his own?"

"Very hard. I called him every night for weeks to make sure Randy was doing his job. Mark finally got sick of it and told me to stop. It was difficult, but I did it. Children must grow up. Even sick ones."

April averted her gaze. Her parents loved her too, but they hadn't learned how to let go of her yet. "I wish my parents felt that way."

"They'll change their minds. That day your mother came to talk to me, I could see how much she loved you. She knows that your life with Mark won't be easy, and she doesn't want you to get in over your head."

"But it's my head," April insisted. "I'm sorry if she bothered you."

"She didn't. She was only trying to figure out what you were up against if you married my son. I was honest with her. I told her it wasn't going to be easy, but that I thought you had what it took to deal with Mark's illness."

"You did?" Her compliment pleased April.

"Of course. You're bright and mature. And you know what it is to live with medical uncertainty."

Truthfully, April hadn't thought much about her own problem since the day she'd rushed out of Dr. Sorenson's office. As long as her tumor was dormant, she saw no purpose in dwelling on it. And if it did start growing again, well . . . she figured she'd worry about it at that time. "I really love Mark," she told his mother. "I know a lot of people think we shouldn't get married, but I honestly believe we can make a life for ourselves. Just as long as we're together."

Rosa smiled. "I always knew that it would

take a very special girl to love Mark. When Mark was growing up I lit candles in church every Sunday and prayed that God would find such a girl for him."

April returned Rosa's smile. "I don't know if Mark told you, but my parents went through a lot to conceive me. Mom told me that she's always looked forward to having a grandchild to spoil."

Rosa stiffened, and her eyes grew guarded. "Y-You want children?"

Mark's mother looked visibly upset. April couldn't understand her reaction. "Well . . . sure . . . I guess so." Still, Rosa stared at her silently, and April began to feel unsure of herself. "Oh, not right away, of course. I—I mean, we'd wait awhile. Are you afraid we might pass on bad genes to our kids?"

Before Rosa could answer, Mark walked into the room, and both women turned toward him. "What's wrong?" He glanced anxiously from his mother to April.

"April has just told me she might like to have a child," Rosa said, reproach in her voice.

Mark's face flushed crimson.

"What's wrong?" April asked, suddenly

feeling like a person who'd walked into the middle of a play without knowing her lines.

"I . . . ," Mark began, stopped, then said, "We have to talk."

"Yes," his mother said. "You have to talk. And shame on you, son, for waiting until now to talk to April about this."

"Please," April pleaded. "Will someone please tell me what's going on?"

Rosa said, "I'll leave the two of you alone," and quickly left the room.

With her heart pounding, April stepped closer to Mark, waiting for him to say something.

When he looked at her, pain was etched into his face. "I can't give you babies, April. Not ever."

18

"You don't want children?"

"I didn't say I didn't want them. I said I couldn't have them."

April couldn't grasp what he was trying to tell her. "But why?"

Mark's eyes clouded. "It's the CF. Guys who have CF are sterile. We can never father children."

April felt as if she'd been kicked in the stomach. *How could it?* she wondered. "I didn't know."

He held her eyes with his gaze. "Does it make a difference?"

"I'm not sure," April answered slowly. "Having babies isn't something I've thought a lot about. I mean, my friends and I used to talk about it. Once, one of my friends thought she might be pregnant. It turned out that she wasn't, but it really made me stop and think what it would be like to have a baby."

"Well, you'll never have to worry about an unwanted pregnancy with me. That's for sure." Mark sounded bitter. "But please tell me if it's going to make a difference for us. If children are so important that you no longer want to marry me."

April chose her words carefully. "What bothers me *most* is that you didn't tell me."

"When would I have?"

"When you gave me the ring?"

He gave a short humorless laugh. "Sure. That would have made the night memorable: 'Will you marry me, and oh, by the way, I can't ever have kids.'"

"Mark, once I saw all your medicine bottles, the oxygen tank, all that stuff—well, that might have been a perfect time to have had a heart-to-heart about CF. I asked you to let me learn how to do your thumps, and at first you said no. You've had plenty of chances to talk about it."

"I didn't want to lose you."

"Well, if that was going to break up our

relationship, then we didn't have much going for us, did we?" she asked quietly.

He rubbed his eyes with the heel of his palm, and when he looked at her, he looked ashamed. "I underestimated you, April."

"You've done that a lot."

"I'm sorry."

She felt tears sting her eyes. "I'm sorry too, Mark. I'm sorry you didn't trust me enough to be honest."

He squared his shoulders and hooked his thumbs in the pockets of his jeans. "I never wanted anything as much as I wanted you. The odds are pretty good that you'll outlive me, April." He raised a hand to stop her protest. "No, hear me out. It's the truth and we both know it. I'm not afraid of dying, but there's a lot of living I want to do before death catches up with me. *You* are part of that living. I want you. I have from the first time I saw you. But if having children is a dream of yours, I can't give it to you, no matter how much I want to."

In that moment, April saw her life stretching in front of her without Mark. The image was so bleak, she shuddered. Losing him eventually was inevitable. Nothing could stop it from happening. But she couldn't let him go now, not under any circumstances. With a catch in her voice, she said, "The only thing that's important to me is loving you."

He closed the space between them with a long stride and took her in his arms. "I love you, April. I love you more than anything in this world."

When her mother returned from her trip, April decided she would have to discuss the wedding with her, whether her mother wanted to hear it or not. She wanted her mother's help. She *needed* her mother's help.

So one bright October afternoon, April stopped at the antique store. She opened the door. A bell tinkled delicately and the scent of old furniture, lemon oil, and silver polish hung in the air. She loved the store. When she had been a little girl, she used to go to work with her mother and play among the antique furniture. Tapestries hung on walls alongside gilded sconces. There were expensive Oriental carpets, armoires, richly carved chairs, and old-world furniture that turned the floor space into a wonderful maze. Overhead a series of crystal chandeliers, some more than a hundred years old, evoked images of elegant ballrooms and velvet gowns. Tables were draped with fine lace and crisp linen and held ornate silver bowls, fine English porcelain, and cut crystal vases filled with bouquets of freshly cut flowers.

"April! How nice to see you," Caroline, her mother's partner, called out. "How are you?"

April embraced the slender brown-haired woman. "I'm fine. The shop looks wonderful."

"Thanks to your mother. She's found some positively fabulous Shaker-style furniture. She's in the back inventorying it right now. She tells me you're getting married. Congratulations."

April was surprised that Caroline announced the news so happily. "Thanks."

"I'm so pleased for you. You look around the shop and pick out a gift for yourself. Anything you want." Caroline patted her arm.

Caroline's offer stunned April. She hadn't expected her to be so enthusiastic, especially knowing the way her mother felt. "Thank you! I'll bring Mark some afternoon and we'll choose something together."

"April!" Her mother came out of the store's back room.

"Hi, Mom."

Caroline said, "You two visit and I'll go work on the inventory."

Once they were alone, April's mother asked, "What brings you here?"

"I was doing some wedding dress shopping and thought I'd stop by." She hated that her tone sounded challenging, but she couldn't help it.

"Have you found something you like?"

"Actually, I have. Several, in fact. I need another opinion."

"Would you like mine?"

April held her breath, hoping that she and her mother could come to terms. She didn't like being at odds with her parents. "Yes. I'd like yours very much."

Her mother walked to the back of the store and minutes later returned with her trench coat. "I told Caroline I wouldn't be back today."

"Are you sure?"

Their gazes locked. "My only daughter is getting married soon. I can't let any opportunity go by to help with her wedding." Her mother hugged April, then held her at arm's length. Her mother's eyes shimmered.

A lump rose in April's throat. She realized how much it meant to her to have her mother's support—even a little. "Thanks, Mom."

"So do you have any particular dress you'd like to show me first?" Her mother opened the door, and the bell sounded its silvery notes.

"There's one in a shop six blocks away."

"Let's go look at it. Shall I grab us a cab?"

April smiled, looped her arm through her mother's, and said, "It's a beautiful day. Let's walk."

Together they headed down the crowded sidewalk, the crisp October afternoon fairly crackling around them.

Her parents' unexpected support was a wonderful and welcome surprise. They threw themselves wholeheartedly into planning her wedding. "Can we stick to some kind of a budget?" April's father asked cautiously.

April and her mother looked at each other and burst out laughing. "A budget!" her mother exclaimed. "Oh, really, Hugh, you're so funny. I wouldn't dream of sticking to a budget."

He groaned, and April winked at him, as if to say, *It's okay, Daddy. I won't go crazy on you.*

April's and Mark's parents met to discuss plans and sort through details. April and Mark decided to take them to their favorite restaurant early on the afternoon of Mark's final race for the season. "We'll eat, attack the wedding plans, then we'll all go to the track together," Mark declared.

"I know I can get my parents to go to the track," April told him, "but can you persuade your mother?"

"She's already agreed. She's not turning handsprings, mind you, but she wants to make a good impression on your parents. Refusing to go with the rest of us might be interpreted the wrong way."

So they all arrived at the track together. Mark's father was talkative and beaming; his mother looked nervous. April's parents were curious to see firsthand Mark's obsession with fast cars. Once they were settled in the grandstands, April went down on the infield, where

Mark was climbing into his birthday coveralls. "You look just like a pro," she said, checking him over from head to toe.

"Thanks to you. At least the weather's cooled off. These things are hot." He tucked his helmet under his arm.

"I'm glad you're driving in the first heat. I don't think your mother can stand too much of this."

"Well, if I win, everyone still has to stick around for the finals."

"I'll make sure no one bolts."

He leaned forward and kissed the tip of her nose. "You're one in a million."

"Just remember that when you discover I can't cook."

He untied her scarf and retied it around his arm. "For luck."

She smiled. "See you in the winner's circle."

Back in the stands, April had to shout to be heard above the roar of the cars as they looped the track, waiting for the green flag to drop. She felt a surge of pride as Mark's car nosed a path through the staggered string of starters.

The flag dropped and the cars shot forward. April heard her father shout, "Go for it!"

"It's awesome, huh?" she yelled above the roar of the engines as the cars rocketed around the track. "Keep your eye on Mark and watch how he snakes out the other drivers," she yelled in her mother's ear. "He's really good at this."

She watched expectantly as Mark drafted behind the leader, knowing that in a split second he would floor the accelerator and zip past his opponent. She saw him make his move. But suddenly the lead car swerved. Its engine made a popping sound, and smoke billowed from beneath its hood. She heard Mark's father shout, "The guy's blown an engine!"

She leaped up, watching in horror, as Mark's car clipped the other car's back fender. Mark's car spun out of control, slammed into the retaining wall, flipped, and caught fire.

19

April paced the floor of the emergency room like a caged animal. She couldn't sit still or close her eyes because whenever she did, visions of the past few hours flooded her mind.

She saw Mark's car in flames, men scrambling onto the track with fire extinguishers and then prying open the crumpled door of Mark's car, hauling out his limp body, and a fire-rescue truck speeding him away. Mark had been flown in a helicopter to the huge medical complex in the city, where they all now waited for word of his condition.

With a start, April realized that she'd come full circle—back to the very hospital where Mark had first walked into her room months before and announced, "You're the girl I'm going to marry." Silently she begged, *Please, God, please let him be all right.*

April couldn't stand seeing Mark's mother, sitting ramrod straight in a chair, never moving, not even flinching. All her fears had been realized that night in front of her eyes. And nothing her husband could say brought her any peace. Anything Mr. Gianni said was greeted with a stony silence from Mark's mother that was as impenetrable as a wall. It broke April's heart.

At some point, Mark's sisters arrived in a rush of tears and fell into their mother's arms. Her own parents were troupers, going for coffee and sodas, calling friends and family. "I'll get us a room at a nearby hotel," April's father offered.

April insisted that she wasn't going to leave the hospital, so he'd be wasting his money. And just when she didn't think she would be able to bear the suspense one more minute, a doctor appeared and hustled them into a corner of the waiting room.

"How is he?" Mark's father asked, taking his wife's hand.

April braced herself for the worst.

"He's doing remarkably well," the doctor said, and April felt her knees go weak. "He has a broken foot, three cracked ribs, and first- and second-degree burns on the side of his face and on his left hand. It's very fortunate that he was wearing that flame-retardant suit. It saved his life."

Mark's parents turned to her and she read gratitude in their eyes. Mark was alive! "Can we see him?" April asked.

"I'm having him moved upstairs to a room. He's being sedated so he'll rest more comfortably. You can see him there."

"How soon before we can take him home?" Rosa asked.

"That will be up to the endocrinologist, Dr. Bejar. He'll take over your son's case. Just because Mark's injuries weren't severe doesn't mean he won't need careful monitoring. The suit protected him from burns, but it did little to protect his lungs from smoke inhalation. He's not out of the woods yet."

It was well after midnight before Mark was settled into a room and April and both families could see him. The head of his bed had been raised so that he was semi-upright. The side of his face and his hand were wrapped in gauze and his foot, encased in a soft cast, rested on a pillow. His chest had been wrapped in tape to keep his torso rigid, and an oxygen mask was strapped across his mouth.

His mother and sisters broke down crying. "I'm all right," he told them. "Just banged up. Don't cry." He appeared exhausted and his speaking was laborious, but his gaze kept falling on April.

It seemed like forever before she was alone with him. With her parents waiting in the hall, she leaned over him, slid her arms around him, and rested her head on his shoulder. "I thought I'd lost you," she whispered.

"No . . . such . . . luck," he said with difficulty.

She wiped away the tears sliding down her cheeks. "You need to rest. Dad's forcing me to go to a hotel, but I'll be back first thing in the morning."

"Love you."

She kissed him tenderly. "I love you too. Now get some rest."

He was asleep before she left the room.

By the next day, Mark's color had returned. The oxygen mask had been traded for small oxygen tubes clamped to his nostrils, which allowed him to talk more easily. Still, his voice sounded thick and scratchy to April.

"You gave us all a real scare," she told him after a hug and a kiss.

"Please, I've already heard all about it from my mother."

Rosa had left the room to give Mark and April privacy, but April hadn't been surprised to learn that she'd spent the entire night in the chair by her son's bed. "Are you in any pain?"

"My side's killing me, but don't let my mother know. I told her I feel pretty good. Actually I feel like I was dragged behind my car."

"It was so awful, Mark." April shook her head. The memory still haunted her. "I can't get over the picture of your car overturning and going up in flames."

"Don't think about it. I've called the garage to see how much damage was done to the car. And to get estimates on repairs. It's more work than I can do by myself—"

"You're not really going to race that thing again, are you?"

"I sure am. But not until after we're married. I promise not to do anything to threaten our wedding again." He grinned.

Upset, she cried, "It's not our wedding I worry about, Mark. It's your life!"

"I can't fight about this now."

He coughed deeply and harshly. The sound chilled her. She immediately backed away from her argument. "You're right, this isn't the time to go into this. Just put all your energy into getting well."

He took several labored breaths before he asked, "Have you found a dress yet?"

She jumped at the chance to change the subject. "I think so. It's beautiful, Mark. Kind of simple, but with a long train that's decorated with lace and seed pearls. The store's altering it for me." He nodded and smiled, but she could tell he was weak and tired. "Listen, I'm going to run down to the cafeteria, but I'll be back soon."

He didn't protest, and she hurried into the hall, where she discovered Rosa huddled in a discussion with a dark-haired man in a white lab coat. Rosa introduced April to Dr. Bejar as Mark's fiancée, and the doctor greeted her cordially. "It's good to meet you. I'm sorry it has to be under these conditions."

"How's Mark? I mean how is he *really*?"

Dr. Bejar glanced at Rosa, who gave him a silent nod of assent. Dr. Bejar said, "I'm concerned about his CF. The smoke he inhaled is bad enough, but the broken ribs make it extremely difficult to maintain his daily therapy and break up the congestion."

April hadn't even considered that Mark's broken ribs could be a threat to his health. Suddenly frightened, she asked, "What are you going to do?"

"That's what Mrs. Gianni and I were just discussing. I can insert a drainage tube through his chest and into his lung and increase his decongestant and inhalant medications. I want to keep pneumonia at bay, because frankly, it's a serious risk for him."

Pneumonia. April felt afraid. For Mark. For herself. For all their plans and dreams.

"He's a good doctor," Rosa said once Dr. Bejar had gone. "We trust him completely to do what's best for Mark."

"I just want him to get well."

Rosa touched her April's arm. "Me too, April. Me too."

The minor surgery to insert the drainage tube was performed without complications, and Mark was moved into intensive care. April stayed with him as much as the hospital rules allowed and was astounded at how many hospital personnel stopped by to see him once word spread that he was there. Rosa explained, "Mark's been a patient here off and on for many years. These people have come to know him and truly care about him."

Once news got around about Mark, he had a steady stream of visitors—nurses, health care professionals, friends he'd made in the hospital during his frequent stays over the years. April realized that to many of them, Mark was a CF patient who'd, so far, beaten the odds. She only hoped he could do it one more time.

April's mother continued with the wedding plans, partly to give April something else to occupy her mind. When she could pry April away from the hospital, they visited stationery stores and flipped through books of sample invitations. They checked out florists, listening to suggestions for flowers and greenery for the June date April and Mark had chosen. They sampled the wares of bakeries and caterers, and April became entranced by photos of elaborate cakes.

April found herself caught between the dreamworld of a fantasy wedding and the harsh reality of the hospital and sickness. Mark always seemed heartened when she told him about the wedding plans, so she kept working on them. But after he had spent a week in the hospital with no obvious improvement, she began to see his enthusiasm fading and his hope crumbling.

He said, "I'm never going to get out of here."

"Don't talk that way. Of course you will. Dr. Bejar said you shouldn't put a time limit on this stay. Your injuries—"

"Aren't getting better," Mark finished. "I don't want to be pushed down the aisle in a wheelchair, April."

"It's only November. We have months until the wedding." She fingered the chain around her neck, the half of a heart he'd given her. "Besides, my father will strangle you if you break off our engagement."

He managed a half smile. "That will never happen. But if you want to—"

"Stop it!" Her voice was sharp. "I won't

listen to you say those things. I plan to marry you in June, so get used to the idea."

His expression turned grave. "April, I once told you I wasn't afraid of dying. That's a lie. I used to not be scared, but that was before I met you and made all these plans for living. No matter what happens, remember, I love you. And this past spring and summer have been the happiest of my life. All because of you."

"Mark, please, don't give up."

"I can't help it. I know how I feel physically. I know that somehow, this time, it's different."

April tried to change the subject and make him laugh. But Mark was right. That night he developed a fever and pneumonia.

20

"He's on the strongest antibiotic available." Dr. Bejar was updating both families about Mark's condition. "I've ordered a morphine infusion pump too. This way, whenever he's in pain, he can administer a small dose himself."

"But he will get better," April blurted out. "I mean, with this antibiotic, he will get over his pneumonia."

Mark's mother added, "You've always been honest with us, Dr. Bejar. Please don't hold anything back now. We want to know the truth."

The doctor looked serious. "Rosa, his lungs have been badly scarred by years of living with

CF. I can't make any predictions at this time. Let's just take it day by day."

April felt sick to her stomach and didn't dare look at Mark's parents. If she did, she was certain she would crumble. She felt weary, like a swimmer treading water. Her life had been put on hold, and she'd become so caught up in Mark's situation that she felt as if her whole existence revolved around the routine of the hospital. She had dropped her classes at NYU, telling her parents, "I can't concentrate on college."

"How are you feeling?" her mother had asked. "Perhaps you should see Dr. Sorenson. All this stress—"

April had glared at her. "This isn't about me. I'm fine and I don't want Mark thinking about anything except getting well. I'm not leaving this hospital until he does."

After Dr. Bejar left them, April found a quiet corner, took her father's cell phone, and with trembling fingers dialed Kelli's dorm room in Oregon. She'd talked to Kelli twice since Mark's accident, but now more than ever, she wanted to hear her friend's voice. With a three-hour time difference, it wasn't always easy to catch her in but, miraculously, Kelli answered on the second ring. April poured out her story through tears. "He's so sick, Kelli. He's really bad."

"Hey, I have faith in medical science. And besides, I want to be your maid of honor."

She knew Kelli was trying to cheer her up by focusing on the wedding, but it wasn't working. "There isn't going to be any wedding if Mark . . ." She couldn't bring herself to finish the sentence.

"Listen," Kelli said, quickly covering the awkwardness. "I bought myself a beeper. That way you can reach me anytime." She gave April her number.

"I miss you, Kelli. I wish you were here."

"Me too, April. I'd be there in an instant, if I could." April heard tears of regret in her friend's voice. There was nothing Kelli could do, nothing any of them could do except wait. April hung up and returned to the ICU.

The hospital kept several guest rooms for family members of patients in the ICU. April and Rosa moved into one, a cubicle with twin cots, a single dresser, and a bathroom. April's parents kept their hotel suite. Mark's father and sisters stayed at the family house. That way they could be near the hospital.

Mark's breathing became so labored that it hurt April physically to hear him struggle to breathe. Forming words, saying sentences was nearly a superhuman feat, and she tried as much as possible to keep him from speaking. But he struggled valiantly to talk to her, to his family. Every time he saw her, he rasped, "Love . . . you."

After four days on antibiotics, he was no better. April longed to make time stand still, but realized that even if she had the power to make it happen, she didn't have the heart to watch Mark continue to suffer. She took his hand, and when he urged her closer, she bent over his bed, placing her ear near his mouth. "I'm sorry . . . I . . . tried . . . but . . . I can't . . . ," he rasped.

Tears blurred her eyes. "What can I do for you?"

"Live . . . for us. I . . . wish I . . . could have seen you . . . as my bride."

Mark's parents came in his room to be with him, and April went to her father. "Daddy, I need your and Mom's help."

"Anything."

"Please, go get my wedding dress. I know it's not ready yet, but I don't care. Just bring it to me."

April heard the serious tone of her own quavering voice. Her father hugged her quickly and left immediately. Her mother asked, "What can I do?"

"Nothing just now," April told her.

April brooded and paced the floor, overcome with a sense of urgency. Rosa found her and said, "I'm calling our priest, April. I want Mark to have last rites."

April felt icy cold and numb with pain. "I understand," she said.

When her parents returned with a huge box, April took her mother into the tiny room she shared with Mark's mother, and there, she tugged on crinolines, slip, and the gorgeous ivory satin gown. Working hurriedly, her mother tucked and pinned, fitting the dress to April's slim body as best she could. "I have no veil," April moaned as she looked in the mirror.

Her mother left but soon returned with a makeshift wreath of baby's breath and a hastily tied-together bouquet. "I swiped these from every floral arrangement I could get my hands on." She handed April the bouquet and settled the wreath into her mane of thick red hair, pinning it securely.

April's hands shook, and she bit her lip hard to keep tears back. "I can't go into that room crying," she explained.

Her mother fluffed April's long dress and through her own tears said, "You look beautiful."

April left the small room. Nurses, lab technicians, and even office personnel had formed a line down the corridor. She questioned her father with her eyes and he shrugged, saying, "I don't know how word spread, but it did."

She walked toward Mark's cubicle, the exquisite train of the gown sweeping the floor behind her while the onlookers quietly watched. "You are perfectly beautiful," said one of Mark's favorite nurses. "And what you're doing is wonderful."

At the door, April saw the priest leaning over Mark, his prayer book open. Her knees almost buckled. She felt her father take her arm. "I think it's customary for a bride to be given away by her father," he said.

Together they entered the room. Startled, the priest and Mark's parents looked up, and upon seeing April, Rosa's expression passed from grief to gratitude. They stepped aside, and April moved to the bed. Softly she called Mark's name. She was dry-eyed now, and calm.

She saw his eyelids flutter open, his brown eyes widen, and his mouth turn up in a smile. "Beautiful . . ."

She smiled back, laid aside her bouquet, and took his unbandaged hand. " 'Until death do us part,' " she whispered.

"Until . . . paradise," he answered.

"I love you."

But Mark was beyond hearing.

April passed trancelike through the next few days. At the funeral home viewing, her parents stood on either side of her, supporting her while she stood over Mark's satin-lined casket and looked down at his body. *Not Mark,* she told herself. Only a waxen shell. He wore his racing suit, and April realized how much strength it had taken for Rosa to allow it. Rosary beads were wrapped around his hand, and dangling from a chain around his neck was the half heart he'd carried on his key chain since the day he'd given April hers. She unfastened from her neck the chain that held her matching half of the heart and dropped it into the casket.

The day of the funeral was cold, and the sun played hide-and-seek with the clouds, casting dappled shadows over the cemetery. After the mass at Mark's church, April rode with Mark's family in a black limousine to the graveside, telling herself that it would all be over soon. That she only had to make it one more minute, then the next minute, and then the one after that. Exactly how Mark had taught her to live her life.

Afterward she went to Mark's parents' home, where family and friends gathered to eat and reminisce about Mark. She thought about the first time Mark had brought her here to meet his family. And about the last time for his birthday party.

She returned home with her parents and, once in her room, stripped and crept beneath the covers. There, in the quiet darkness, she called Kelli out in Oregon. "It's over," April said.

"I wanted to be with you so bad."

April could hear that Kelli had been crying. "It's okay, Kelli. You'll be home for Christmas and maybe I'll be better company by then."

"I just want you to be all right."

"I don't know how to be 'all right,' Kelli. Mark was *everything* to me. And now he's gone. Now, I'm alone. All alone."

Darkness as heavy as New York's winter snow settled over April. All around her the city dressed up for the holidays. Store windows bloomed with festive Christmas scenes. Lights, glittery trees, and bell-ringing Santas were everywhere. But April found no joy or peace or comfort in any of it. Wherever she went, wherever she looked, she was bombarded with memories of Mark.

When she went for her checkup with Dr. Sorenson, it took every ounce of strength and courage to walk back inside the hospital. He took X rays and told her, "You're holding your own. The tumor's dormant. If you continue to feel good, I'll see you in three months."

The good news didn't mean anything to her. Her head was all right, but her heart was broken. It wasn't fair.

She went to her father one December afternoon and spread out travel brochures on the desk in front of him. "Daddy, remember these?"

"Yes, from when you graduated."

"Well, now I want to go away. I want us to take that trip you promised."

"Where would you like to go?"

She shrugged. "It doesn't matter. Someplace where it isn't winter."

He pondered her request. "It will take a little time for your mother and me to get things organized here."

"That's fine."

"Are you sure you don't have a destination in mind?"

She shook her head. "You and Mom pick. Just make sure it's warm. I miss the summer, Daddy. I'm so tired of being cold."

21

The villa, nestled high above a cove on a hill on the island of St. Croix in the Virgin Islands, faced the ocean. Cool tropical breezes, fragrant with the aromas of exotic flowers and tangy ocean air, stirred through the wide-open doors and windows. April's bedroom faced west, toward the water, so that the first and last things she saw morning and night were the vivid turquoise waters of the Caribbean and a sweep of blue sky. Sunsets painted the sky coral and red, pink and lavender. Sometimes, when she woke in the middle of the night, moonlight cut a path across the dark face of the sea. Under the spell of the water's eternal beauty, April felt the winter cold inside her slowly begin to thaw.

Surrounding the villa were gardens, lush with thick tropical foliage with wondrous names like hibiscus, bougainvillea, oleander. The house was isolated, the only road to it narrow and winding. Weathered wooden stairs led down from the house to the white sandy cove. April went down to the beach every day, and there she read or simply sat staring out at the sea, remembering. Sometimes she cried. More often, she simply marveled at the way the sound and smell of the island eased the tightness in her chest and soothed the pain in her heart. St. Croix had been the perfect choice.

"I've taken the house for six months," her father had told her while they were still in New York. "And I can get an extension."

"That's so long!" April exclaimed. "How can you and Mom take the time?"

"I told Caroline I'd do some island-hopping and exploring," her mother said with a smile. "Who knows what treasures I'll find?"

April's father insisted, "I can keep in touch with my office via fax, phone, and modem. If I have to go back, I can fly out and be in New York in hours."

April was grateful. She loved St. Croix and

decided that when she felt up to it, she'd go scouting. The island had originally been settled by the Danish. It was twenty-three miles long, with the old city of Christiansted on one end and Frederiksted at the other, and a tropical rain forest between them. St. Croix would have been the perfect place for a honeymoon.

One day April awoke and the sea stretched out glassy calm below her window, the sun sparkled brilliantly, and puffy white clouds floated like cotton candy pillows in the sky. She knew the time had come.

She pulled on shorts and hiking boots and started up the green hill behind the house. The going was rough, but she made it to the top and stood, gazing out at the water, which was dotted with an occasional sailboat. She lifted her face skyward and spun in a circle, her arms flung open as if to hug the breeze. Up on this hill, she felt closer to heaven, and closer to Mark. Remembering her mission, she stopped.

She reached into her pocket, brought out a single red balloon, put it to her lips, and began to puff. Slowly it filled and rounded out. She tied it, reached again into her pocket, and removed a long strand of yellow ribbon. She tied it securely to the balloon and waited for a breeze.

When the breeze blew, soft and balmy from the sea, April flung the balloon upward, shielded her eyes from the sun's glare, and held her breath. She watched as the air current caught it and pulled it upward. Inside the balloon she'd placed her breath, her kiss of life, as Mark had done for her. She wondered if he could see it, sailing toward him in heaven. April watched until it became no more than a red dot, rising ever higher, as if to touch the sun.

To find out what happens to April Lancaster,
turn the page for a sneak preview
of Lurlene McDaniel's companion book,
For Better, for Worse, Forever

April downshifted, and the Jeep wound its way
along the coastal highway. Armed with maps
of St. Croix and caution from her parents,
she'd headed east, repeating to herself her
mother's anxious warning, "Remember, stay
left. Stay left."

Wind whipped through her hair as she
bounced along the curving highway. As she
rounded bends in the road, she glimpsed sight
of the jewel-blue Caribbean, an occasional
rocky cliff, and lush green distant hills. Sun
beat down on her arms and shoulders, and the
intoxicating smell of salt air mingled with the
sweet aroma of flowers. The roads were few in
the island, and now, in the height of tourist
season, not heavy with traffic. She gripped the
wheel and stepped on the accelerator, as she
remembered when Dr. Sorenson said that despite weeks of radiation treatments, the tumor
entrenched in her cerebellum and brain stem
had not shrunk as hoped. He was so, so sorry.
There was little else medical science could do
for her.

Understanding her anguish at the time,
Mark had taken her out to a deserted airstrip

and told her to drive his car as fast and as hard as she wanted. And she had forced his fine old car to its optimum speed and experienced the dangerous but exhilarating balance between control and oblivion. It had been a gift that only Mark could have given her, because he was the only one who understood what it was like to live one's life with the ever-present specter of death on high.

Mark would have loved St. Croix. He would have sped along the back roads and climbed trails where only four-wheel-drive vehicles ventured. They would have had such a good time together. A mist of tears clouded her eyes, and she slowed down the Jeep.

She glanced to one side and saw a large sign: THE BUCCANEER. On impulse, she spun the wheel of the car and drove through the gateway and down a sloping road through acres of rolling green land. The edges of a golf course lay on her right, and far back, on a bluff overlooking the sea, stood a sprawling clubhouse and hotel. She parked in the lot and walked out on a terrace set with tables and chairs. A hostess asked, "Do you have a lunch reservation?"

April cleared her throat and smiled nervously. She had no business being there. "Actually, I was looking for your pro shop."

The hostess directed her there and April hurried out onto the splendid grounds of the luxury resort, down a tiled path to the shop. Once inside, she asked for Brandon, then busied herself among the clutter of golf paraphernalia. She chided herself, saying that what she was doing was stupid. She had no real reason to see Brandon. She hoped that he wasn't there, that this was a Saturday he didn't work. The door opened and she turned to face him across a rack of golf shirts. His face, damp with sweat, broke into a large grin. "I don't believe it! You came to see me!"

She had to laugh at his genuine astonishment. "I was just driving by and saw the sign. I didn't even know if you'd be here."

"I've been here since six A.M. We start early because golfers like to start before it gets hot. I'm about to take a lunch break. Want to eat with me?"

She wasn't hungry, but since she'd come this far and knew she couldn't leave easily she answered, "Maybe a salad."

He took her back to the terrace restaurant, ordered, and had the food packed in Styrofoam containers, then led her down a winding walkway to a sandy beach area. Hotel guests were sunning themselves and playing in the calm waters. He pulled a small table and two chairs around to an alcove of rocks enclosing an isolated strip of sand no larger than a good-sized back porch. "Since the tide's out, we can sit here," he said, planting the chairs firmly in the wet sand. "It's private."

She removed her sandals, allowing the warm water to lap over her feet. He sat across from her so that he was framed by blue sky and bright turquoise ocean. His tanned face glowed and his hair looked golden, streaked by the sun. "I'm starving," he said, flipping open his container and lifting out a mammoth hamburger.

Watching Brandon wolf down his meal reminded her of all the times she'd eaten with Mark. But, of course, before Mark could eat he'd had to take pills because of his CF. She thought of their special restaurant and of their table tucked in the corner.

"What's funny?" Brandon asked. "You

were smiling just then. Have I got mustard smeared on my face?"

She gazed self-consciously at her salad. "I was just remembering something, that's all. Nothing important."

"I'll be honest," he said between bites. "I never thought I'd see you again."

"Me neither."

"I'm glad you changed your mind. Why *did* you change your mind?"

"I didn't know I needed a reason."

"My charming personality?" he offered with an infectious grin.

"Certainly that was part of it." She returned his smile. A gull swooped low over the water behind him. "I was knocking around the island."

"And you thought, *Wonder what old Brandon's up to? Maybe I should go see the geek.*" His tone reminded her of Mark's.

"Actually, I was . . . lonely." She kept her gaze on the gull, unable to meet Brandon's. She hadn't meant to tell him that.

He leaned back in his chair and searched her face thoughtfully. "I figured something was up with you. I've seen you twice and you looked sad both times." She didn't respond, so he continued. "I've been lonely myself, so I know how it feels."

"Everybody's been lonely."

"But you don't have to be," he said. "April, St. Croix is a small place. Everybody knows everybody else, especially those of us who grew up here. Tourists come through all the time, and sometimes the locals hit it off with some of them. We know that the person is going to leave. That's a given. But we still have a good time together while we can, as long as the person is on the island . . ."

She understood what he was trying to tell her—that he would take her under his wing with no strings attached. "Like a baby-sitter?"

"You're no baby," he declared, appraising her in a way that made her pulse flutter. "No. As a friend. This wouldn't be only for you. You see, I could use a friend myself."

"There are plenty of tourists who would jump at the chance to be your friend, Brandon."

"But I don't want just anybody. I'd like it to be you."

The way he kept looking at her made her feel self-conscious. An inner voice asked,

"What are you doing?" Suddenly she saw that she was acting flirty and was instantly ashamed. She struggled to stand, but the wet sand had sucked around the legs of the chair so that it couldn't move. "It's really getting late. I've got to go, and you've got to work."

"Don't go yet." Instantly Brandon was beside her, taking her arm so that she wouldn't trip backward. His touch felt warm, and she pulled away as if it had burned her.

"I have to," she insisted.

"I'd like to see you again. Can I call you? Make a date? I have classes until two, but I'm free evenings. I could show you around St. Croix. Maybe take you over to St. Thomas or St. John."

"I—I don't think so." Despite being in a wide-open space, April suddenly felt hemmed in and claustrophobic. "I really have to go now." She grabbed her sandals and backed away. "Thanks."

"Call me here if you change your mind," he said to her as she ducked around the edge of the rocks and fled up the beach toward the parking lot where her Jeep was parked. With her heart hammering, April turned on the engine and shot up the road to the highway, where she forgot the rule about staying in the left-hand lane and almost had a head-on collision.

Jerking the car back into its proper lane, she sped toward the hills and the safety of the villa. She never should have stopped to see Brandon. Not because she wasn't attracted to him, but because she was. And because she kept thinking about another guy who'd wanted to date her but whom she'd rejected at first— Mark. Until he'd won her over with his winsome smiles and caring love and had swept her heart away. But now Mark was gone, and she couldn't bring him back and she couldn't start with someone else.

She floored the accelerator and raced toward home, memories chasing her like the wind.

"Did you have a good time exploring?"

Her mother's question cut through April's semiconscious state. She'd hurried home, put on her bathing suit, and gone down to the private beach for a swim. The surf felt warm as bathwater, the white sand bottom soft as velvet. She'd swum and floated until she was exhausted, and had finally gone to the beach chair, where she slathered herself with sun cream, stretched out, and dozed, hoping to shut off her thoughts. Her mother had come down, bringing a pitcher of cool lemonade. "It was all right," April answered.

Her mother dragged another chair closer. "Tell me about it."

"Nothing to tell. I drove around, that's all."

She heard her mother sigh. "April, I can't stand this noncommunication between us. I know you're hurting, but we used to talk all the time. Now you hardly speak to me. Can't you tell how this is upsetting me? Don't you even care?"

Guilt mixed with irritation, but she knew her mother was right. Her parents had done plenty for her, and she'd shut them out. Just three months before, she and her mother had been knee-deep in wedding plans, and they'd discussed everything. April struggled to sit upright. "I'm sorry."

"You don't have to be sorry. Just *talk* to me. I love you. I want to help."

"Nothing can help. I can't get on top of this, Mom. I start to feel better and then, *POW*, it hits me like a wall. I miss Mark so much." She took a deep breath. "And every time some guy so much as looks at me, I want to run in the other direction."

Her mother poured April a glass of lemonade, and gulls swooped over the sea, flinging their lonely cries against the sunset-colored sky. "St. Croix is a paradise. It's romantic and makes you want to be with somebody you care about. I understand that."

"But how can I? I feel so guilty to even be thinking about such things."

"I know," her mother said. "I can see it on your face. You feel guilty because you're alive and Mark isn't. And because you want to go on living, as you should."